T0244900

# AT
# MIDNIGHT
# WE
# POSSESS
# THE
# DAMNED

Nick Cato & Andre Duza

DEATH'S HEAD PRESS

Published by Death's Head Press,

an imprint of Dead Sky Publishing, LLC

Miami Beach, Florida

www.deadskypublishing.com

Cover by Ken Miller

Design & Formatting by Apparatus Revolution, LLC

Edited by Anna Kubik

*I wish one of my literary heroes, the late Jack Ketchum (aka Dallas Mayr) was here to see this. He encouraged me (at a convention in Pennsylvania) to write this after we discussed an idea I had for a different kind of "snuff" story. This is for him.*
*—Nick Cato*

*Dedicated to the Satanic Panic of the 70s/80s. Without it this story wouldn't have been possible.*
*—Andre Duza*

# 1

---

As Gary McKay cruised down the FDR Drive, he wondered if he could handle what he was about to witness. Just the sheer coldness of it. The utter lack of remorse in those who perform and peddle it. Or so he assumed. Or would he be forever scarred, haunted by something he could never unsee? He was fidgeting in his seat, drying his hands on his knees to prevent them from slipping from the steering wheel, and then replacing them at ten and two. It was all he could do to remain calm. And it wasn't working.

Gary turned on the radio. He fingered the preset channels until something struck him, and when it did, he cranked the volume and spent exactly four minutes and eleven seconds barely distracted from his thoughts by Berlin's *The Metro*. More than the song, Gary had a thing for the 80s, particularly as it related to horror cinema, so the nostalgic vibes it inspired were somewhat medicinal.

As he passed the East 23rd Street exit, that letter, that *goddamn letter* from twelve-years-ago, reared its ugly head again and distracted him from his day-dreaming of what pleasures and horrors the evening might have in store for him. Soon it was all he could think about, despite his best efforts to will it back into the vault of painful memories. He had read the letter so many times it recited itself. As an added kick-in-the-balls, his brain cast the festival Grand Marshall, Salvatore Goldman, who wrote the damn thing, to narrate in his nasally Queens accent.

*DEAR MR. MCKAY:*

*THANK you for your entry in the 14ᵗʰ Annual Brooklyn Horror Film Festival. The competition was fierce this year in our New Director/Short Film category as more entries than ever before were submitted. While your film, DEATH EFFECT, was well received among our judges, we regret to inform you it will not be included in our Top 5 Final Round to be screened this summer at the New York State Horror Film Festival.*

*We wish you much success in placing your short in other festivals, and hope you'll submit again to future Brooklyn Horror Film Festivals.*

*YOURS IN TERROR,*

*SALVATORE GOLDMAN*
  *B.H.F.F. Grand Marshall*

GARY CAUGHT himself speeding and quickly slowed down. That *fucking letter*, and the feelings of disappointment, resentment, and ultimately rage it inspired made his foot heavy and fixed his hands in a white-knuckled-grip on the steering wheel. He loosened them, flexed his fingers one hand at a time, wiped them on his knees, and took a deep, cleansing breath.

Who knew that a fourteen-minute film could have such an

impact? If only he could bottle that power and somehow translate it to the audience through the viewing experience.

*What audience?* sneered the cynical voice in Gary's head.

It had taken him over five years to get the film the way he wanted. He had sacrificed time, and money he had saved from as far back as high-school-graduation, having forfeited the new car his parents had planned to give him in lieu of the equivalent in funds to get his first serious film project off the ground.

He had put in his 10,000 hours, bled, sweated, and cried over his creation, and he was so fucking certain that it would all pay off in the end. He could still remember the swell of enthusiasm that he felt at the time. Even now, the thought of it gave him goosebumps.

Gary chuckled under his breath and shook his head at his naivete.

Most of the films in the final round of the festival ran the gamut of utter shit; from boring, to pretentious, to completely devoid of talent. That these crap-fests were chosen over his mini-epic was a crime and, he was convinced, that the judges' decision had more to do with politics than actual filmmaking skills.

The whole thing had left a stain on his psyche that he had yet to wash away, even after all these years.

Gary recentered his focus as he took the Hamilton Avenue exit into Red Hook, a town that, despite the shiny-happy-hipster gentrification, still contained some seedy spots and businesses.

He preferred the grit and the grime of old as he felt that it had more character. That aesthetic had been used to great effect by some of his favorite directors. Ferrara. Cohen. Henenlotter. To name a few. It had, in turn, influenced his own filmmaking style.

As the scenery on the other side of the windshield melted from shiny-happy to hold-onto-your-purse sketchy, Gary hoped that what he was about to witness wasn't some kind of elaborate hoax. Perhaps it would even reignite the creative spark in him that had extinguished long ago.

~

THE SELECTION WAS a lot larger than he'd expected, although he was still skeptical any were real. Gary thumbed through the box of DVDs, none of which had anything on the clear covers besides a number written in black marker—2, 113, 79, 6, 11, 42, 108. He wanted to know what the numbers meant but decided to keep skimming, not sure what he was looking for.

Then the man who met him at Stor-Ur-Self spoke. "One through forty are adults. Forty-one through Sixty are teenagers. Sixty-one through Seventy are couples, gay and straight. Seventy-one through eighty are seniors. You'd be surprised how well those sell." After lighting a cigarette and smoothing down his beard, he continued. "Eighty-one through one hundred are combos of everything before it and cost a lot more. One-o-one through one-ten are kids. Not only can you probably not afford those, you probably don't want to see 'em."

"I saw a one-thirteen," Gary said. "What's that?"

"You really wanna know?"

After being told he had footage of kids being killed, Gary wondered what could possibly be worse. Of course, he had to know. "I do."

The man removed DVD number 113 and said, "One-eleven to one-twenty is clergy. We have ministers from Catholic, Protestant, Muslim, Hindu, Jewish, and even a few lesser-known groups. Expensive as shit, but as you can see this is the last one. And I don't get new ones in this category too often."

This guy was either the greatest salesman in the history of salesmen or he was running the ultimate scam, and his buddies were about to come out and rob him at any second and probably kick his ass, if not kill him. Gary felt the hunting knife strapped to his ankle and was extra happy he decided to bring it.

"Who's on that one?"

The man laughed. "Son, you'd better show me some cash. If I told you what this'll cost, you wouldn't believe me."

Gary pulled out a wad of one-hundred-dollar bills. Six-grand worth.

The man looked the stack over. "Okay. You sure you want to hear it?"

Gary nodded.

"This here is a Catholic priest. But this is no South American, grainy bullshit. This fucker used to work in a small parish in South Central LA. He was accused of child molestation and had been bounced around the whole country. He won't be missed."

*A priest.* Dear God, Gary thought. *They had a video of a priest being murdered.*

And he *had* to see it.

"You interested?"

"Shit yes, I'm interested."

The man handed the DVD to Gary. "Ready for the rules?"

Gary nodded as his back began to sweat.

"Five G's. Cash. One viewing at another location to be named. You come alone. You watch it once. You pay before the video starts. You leave the second it ends. You keep your mouth shut, or they'll be finding you in about twenty states."

The man stared Gary down in complete sincerity.

Gary nodded yet again.

"Good. You'll be hearing from me within a week. This is done on my time. Understood?"

"Understood."

"If you tell me you can't be there when I say to, the deal is off and you'll have to try to find me again, which won't be as easy as you may think, despite finding me this time. Understood?"

"I'll be there."

Gary fought back asking him if this was real but knew better. If it was a fake video he'd know instantly, considering the countless horror films and online atrocities he had watched over the years. And when he showed up for the screening, he'd make sure his other leg was strapped with his .22. Not the strongest piece in the world but one he wished he had brought now, although as the man took the 113 DVD back and closed the box of discs inside a suitcase, he was glad he didn't.

"You'll be hearing from me within a week. Answer every number that calls because one will be mine," he said.

"Will do."

"Oh, and this will require half the payment now."

"Woah...you expect me to give you twenty-five hundred? Do I look like that much of a schmuck?"

The man took a step toward Gary, smoothed his beard again, and said, "Do you want to see the video?"

Gary remained silent.

"Then that's the gamble you'll have to take. Take it or leave it."

The fucker had the audacity to threaten him out of twenty-five hundred bucks. Gary wanted to stab him and take the whole suitcase, but he still didn't know if they were the only ones in the storage joint.

Shit.

Six months of deep dives into the murky, perverted depths of the dark web to get to this point, and now he was finally at the doors.

*Fuck it*, this shit was *worth* gambling for.

Gary handed the man the requested cash.

The man folded it, slid it in his jacket breast pocket.

"You won't be disappointed. And remember, answer *every* call. One will be me within the next one-to-seven days. Or nights." The man said the last two words with a smirk. "You know the way out?"

"Yes."

"Talk to you soon."

Gary made his way down the dim, fourth-floor hallway, expecting to be jumped at any moment. As a distraction, his mind assigned floating arrows and ethereal text to every doorknob, light-switch, handrail, and elevator button, like items from some catalog of high-touch surfaces to avoid considering the sudden explosion of Hyper Viral Gastroenteritis (aka Hyper VG).

He made it onto the elevator and out into his car without touching a thing, and he didn't see a soul.

Gary pulled out of the Stor-Ur-Self parking lot knowing the man had probably already packed his shit and left, and he had no doubt the room they had met in was gone too or would soon be full of someone else's stuff.

Within minutes Gary was out of Red Hook and decided he needed a drink. His local watering hole was closed by the time he reached Queens, so he decided to call it a night.

Gary took two shots of Jim Beam then brushed his teeth. The liquor made his mouth taste disgusting when combined with the minty toothpaste.

Lying in bed, he hoped he hadn't been scammed and figured if he was, the bastard sure earned his money.

He considered turning on the TV to sidetrack his anxiety, but he'd most likely run into virus coverage at every turn. Even if the media had done as good a job as any horror film he'd seen at stirring up , and sustaining an atmosphere of dread, Gary refused to be an active participant. He preferred to eavesdrop at the watercooler, on elevators, subway cars, and in supermarket check-out lines. As unreliable, misinformed, and oftentimes bat-shit crazy as the theories were, they became colorful fodder to add to the many unfinished script ideas for films he'd likely never make.

And as Gary understood it, the virus was currently restricted to Portsmouth England and a few surrounding cities. Nothing a guy from Flushing to lose any sleep over.

His phone rang before he shut his eyes.

"Meet me at Stor-Right, Thirty-eighth Street in Brooklyn, fourth floor, room sixteen, in forty minutes. No cops. No friends. No bullshit. Got me?"

*Holy shit, it's happening. It's really happening.*

Gary tapped the info into his phone, jumped out of bed and said, "I'm on my way."

# 2

In his excitement, Gary had forgotten about his hunting knife let alone the .22.

His heart beat a bit faster than usual in anticipation of finally seeing an authentic snuff film, so he figured, at this point, that if they were going to rob or kill him, those were the breaks. It wasn't like he had much going on in life, besides a steady diet of horror films, porn videos, and occasionally hooking up with one of the women at the office to assuage his feelings for his ex-girlfriend Karen, whom, by all accounts, he should have married. The thought of being thirty-eight and still single tugged at his pride and his sense of self-worth, but he quickly crushed it down along with any other hope he'd have of ever finding someone else who was into the same crazy shit he was.

But tonight would be worth it. Tonight, he'd be one of the select few who got to see a thing of legend. He'd get to see what others of his ilk had fantasized about since the dawn of film itself, and in that regard, Gary smiled as he checked his slightly graying hair in the rearview mirror.

And as he stepped out of his car, a block away from Stor-Right, Gary rubbed his sweaty hands on his pants and walked forward to what he hoped would be the screening of a lifetime. He felt the lump in his right front pocket, the other half of the admission. Years of saving one hundred here, one hundred there, taking what he could from petty office funds, selling rare books and videos he no longer needed, all added up to this moment.

Gary hadn't passed anyone despite being on a main avenue. His cell phone indicated 5:48, and although cars whizzed by as the rush hour got underway, there seemed to be no foot traffic as he rang the bell located next to two large steel doors.

He was buzzed in. An array of boxes and packing materials filled the first floor of Stor-Right, an elevator on the far wall. His footsteps echoed as he made his way across the cement floor, which reminded him of being in Home Depot. Perhaps this flooring was the industry standard for warehouses. Either way, the elevator was there as soon as he pushed the UP button.

It lifted him noisily to the fourth floor, as if its gears hadn't been oiled since the day it was installed. He took a few deep breaths, trying his best to relax, and by the time the elevator stopped, he was feeling confident.

A sign across the way read *1-8 >> / << 9-16*. Gary stepped into the wide hallway and made a left toward room sixteen. The floor smelled of bleach, which made him wonder whether they were just being fastidious due to the virus, or if they had been up to something far more nefarious.

Two men stood outside the door to room sixteen like urban sentinels: one on either side. Both were easily over six feet tall, and obviously spent most of their time in the gym. The Hispanic man on the right wore a fitted, black tank-top and was covered in tattoos. His eyes hid behind a pair of Ray-Bans despite the hallway not being too bright. The other guy sported lengthy dreadlocks tied neatly behind him in a ponytail. He stepped in front of the door as Gary approached and held out his hand.

"That's far enough, mon," he said with an accent as thick as molasses.

*Jamaican,* Gary thought, knowing full well they were among the last people you'd ever want to fuck with. Not that he'd fuck with anyone here.

He stopped in his tracks and waited. After a few seconds, the Hispanic man walked around Gary and patted him down. Gary was thankful he forgot his knife, although he was sure most people had to have come to these things strapped.

"He's clean," the man said.

"Very good," said the Jamaican. "You have the rest of the money?"

Gary reached into his pocket.

"No, you keep that until he asks for it," he said, referring to the man Gary had met earlier this morning.

"Sorry," Gary replied.

The Jamaican nodded and then opened the door.

"Go in and sit anywhere," the Hispanic man said. His Nuyorican accent was much subtler than the Jamaican's, but equally distinct.

Gary walked past them, briefly worried he'd be cold-cocked the second he did. But the door shut behind him and Gary crossed the large room to the back where three rows of five chairs were set up. A five-foot screen hung from an old-fashioned stand in front. A man, who from behind looked to be in his seventies, sat in the first row. He didn't bother to turn around as Gary approached. Even when Gary took a creaky seat in the third row, the old man stared forward as if the video had already been playing.

Gary sat motionless and silent for five minutes. Then ten. Then fifteen. He grabbed his phone and scrolled through news articles that he couldn't give a shit about to pass the time. Just then, the man from Stor-Ur-Self entered from behind the screen. Gary looked up and realized there was another door he hadn't noticed.

"Glad you gentleman could make it."

He approached the old man with a small cardboard box. "Do you have a phone or any kind of recording device?"

"No."

"Please place the rest of the fee here."

The old man obliged.

The man made his way to the third row and asked the same of Gary.

Gary put his cell in the box, along with the rest of the money, and said, "Just the phone."

"Thank you."

The man placed the box on a table against the wall behind the screen's right side.

"When the film ends, you may take your phone. As soon as you do, you both may leave. And remember what we discussed. The film —the *video,* will begin in a few moments."

Gary figured he changed the word for his benefit, and it gave away the fact he must've been doing this since the days before video became popular. Gary was a true film fanatic, but getting to see what he was about to, in any format, worked for him.

The man removed the cash from the box then left the room and returned two minutes later with a small mobile cart that held a video projector and an older-looking laptop. He wheeled it behind Gary, to the center of the back row, and adjusted the picture to fill most of the five-foot screen. He fidgeted with a few things then made his way to the front of the room as if he was about to address a packed auditorium.

"The video you are about to see is real, and will be seen by your eyes and the eyes of three more people at a later date. This video will then be destroyed."

Gary immediately wondered why this film, which earned $25,000 from a mere five people, would be destroyed if it could make this guy more money. How much had he, or whoever was responsible, been paid to murder this priest, or the people on the other videos?

"We have your address," the man said to the old man, "and yours," he said to Gary. "We know more about the both of you than you think. We trust you will honor my wishes and keep tonight's screenings to yourselves. You will not speak about it, write about it, or ask if others can come see it. Is this understood?"

The old man and Gary said "Yes" in unison.

"Very good."

The man walked to the rear of the room and stood before the digital projector. "Gentleman, this is your one and only chance to leave. If you do, I will return the second part of your fee, but will keep the first."

He waited a few moments. When neither of them stood, he continued.

"Very well."

Gary heard the man take a few steps, and then the lights went out. He stepped back to the projector and said, "Enjoy the show."

The man walked behind the screen and left the room. The video had a few moments of blank filler space. The first image was a wide shot, from some distance, of an old-style church that was badly in need of some TLC. The camera zoomed in, the name of the church intentionally blurred.

After about a minute of slow, sloppy zooming, two men entered the church, quiet, dressed head-to-toe in black, hoodies pulled over their heads, their faces hidden behind clear masks. A third person filmed them from behind as they made their way down the aisle, around the altar area, and into a backroom.

One of the men pounded on a closed office door.

"You here, Padre?"

# 3

O n the ride back to his apartment, Gary felt as if he had
        murdered that priest himself.
            Now that he had seen a genuine snuff film, he wasn't
sure if it was such a good idea. There was a major difference between
watching cheap-looking zombies in Italian films eat people as fake
blood splashed across the screen, and listening to a man plead for his
life as two masked assailants slowly butchered him, right on the altar
where Gary assumed he performed Sunday services.

It wasn't even 8:30, and Gary knew he wasn't heading home. He
had faked a cold on the office voicemail before he left for the screening, so work was out. As much as he hated the job itself, the
Customer Service Department of Bendis/Schlesinger was a tight-knit
cubicle cluster, populated by a colorful cast of characters who
seemed to like him despite his uncompromising horrorphilia.

Although he'd only been there once, a couple years ago, there was
a bar a few blocks from his house that opened at 9:00 for the day
drinkers and bored old men, and he needed a drink or two, or ten,
badly.

When the front door of the Sail Inn opened, Gary waited another
two minutes, then stepped out of his car and crossed the street. The

bartender looked to be in his late sixties, and he barely paid Gary any mind as he took a seat at the center of the bar.

"Be right with ya, buddy," the old man said as he turned the TV on the far wall to a 24-hour news channel featuring a row of fame-whores disguised as pundits stoking fears about Hyper VG.

Gary ordered a shot of Jack, a Jim Beam on the rocks, and a pint of Guinness. The bartender set all three up in front of him and asked if he was going to open a tab or pay. Gary handed him his credit card.

He slammed the shot, took a deep sip of the Jim Beam, then chugged half the pint. The bartender stepped away to finish opening and Gary rested his head in his hands, trying to get the images he had seen earlier out of his mind.

After the two masked men removed the priest's clothes, they had tied him to the altar, facing the seats where the congregation would be seated, and wrapped his mouth in duct-tape. One guy left, and returned with a duffle bag full of power tools and knives.

Gary would never forget the look on the priest's face when one of the killers removed a battery-powered Sawzall, and without hesitation, cut off both of his feet. The combination of disbelief and sheer terror caused the priest to pass out, but they used smelling salts to keep him awake as they cauterized the amputation wounds.

Gary took another pull from the Jim Beam, the ice numbing his lips.

Then, one of the killers used a machete to chop off the priest's hands. His screams were muffled by the duct tape.

The killers mocked his blubbering anguish and stabbed him repeatedly about the legs, arms, and stomach. Just when it seemed the priest was about to lose consciousness for the last time, one of the killers slit him from sternum-to-groin, yanking him alert. The other one grabbed a clutch of his hair and forced him to watch as they pulled out his innards and held them in front of his face.

Gary could tell the exact moment life faded from the priest's bulging eyes, like a light dimming into oblivion. His face, as much of it as was visible above the muzzle of duct-tape, was frozen in a mask of shock. Tears streamed from his eyes even in death, suggesting that his torment was somehow ongoing.

That scared the shit out of Gary. Afterward, the killers tossed the priest's innards to the altar like butchers discarding undesirable cuts of meat.

As Gary finished his pint of Guinness, he wondered how anyone, for any amount of money, could kill someone this way, let alone a priest in his own church. It was obvious these killers were anything but religious, but how could they do this and not feel the slightest bit of remorse?

Or did they?

"You need another?" the bartender asked.

"Please."

As he filled the glass, the bartender asked, "Everything okay, buddy?"

The man's question jolted Gary from his introspection. His response was delayed by a moment of confusion.

"Yeah, thanks. Just had a very rough night."

The bartender took his time leveling off the Guinness, and then went about drying glasses.

Gary was briefly distracted by the TV, where a reporter who looked like Latin Dracula was covering a clash between Curtis Sliwa, the head of the Guardian Angels, and members of a new, religious-themed vigilante group who called themselves the Gatekeepers. With their sleek, white, paramilitary gear and ninja-style masks, the Gate-keepers were more shock-troops targeting drugs and sexualized violence against children than keepers of the peace. Gary had seen their recruitment flyers, which were popping up all over the city.

By the time Gary finished his second pint, there were three other lone, old men in the Sail Inn: two reading the paper, and one sitting two stools down from him, glancing his way, looking for conversation. Gary signaled for the bartender to close his tab. He finished sipping the Jim Beam, and by the time he signed the credit slip he was prop-erly buzzed.

Perhaps he'd be able to get some sleep when he got back to his apartment and sorted out his feelings.

# 4

G ary undressed and made his way to the bedroom in his boxers.

"Long time, no see."

There was a silhouette sitting in the bed-side chair.

"H-how did you get in here?" Gary asked, flicking the light on. It was the man from the screening.

The man smirked as he stood up. Gary interpreted the gesture to mean, *Are you serious*?

Then the man held his hands out in front of him and said, "I washed my hands when I came in."

*Are YOU serious?* Gary thought, the virus being the least of his concerns. The first thing to enter Gary's mind was that the man was here to kill him. He'd just watched a priest get mutilated and murdered, and there was no way these people would let anyone live after seeing it. But as he watched the man admire the professionally framed horror film posters that hung around the room, Gary slowly changed his opinion of the visit.

"I remember when this first came out," the man said, running his right index finger along the frame for an original theater poster of

*Doctor Butcher, M.D.* "I went with a friend to Times Square the first night it screened. Place was packed."

*You have friends?* Gary thought as he took a few deep breaths, doing his best to keep his cool and not try to flee. He also knew, despite the buzz, that this guy would find him wherever he may run to.

"Goofy shit, but the fans seemed to love all those shitty special effects." The man walked over to a framed poster of *Make Them Die Slowly.* "Same with this one. What is it with all you guys and these tribal cannibal movies?"

Gary shrugged his shoulders. "I dunno."

The man shrugged and said "I dunno" mockingly. "After watching a few of these pieces of shit, my friends and I figured we could do better."

The man sat back down, then pointed for Gary to sit on the bed. He listened, vulnerable in nothing but his underwear, and kept calm as the man continued.

"So, what did you think of my film today?"

Gary thought for a moment, then said, "I'm not completely sure yet, but it was a bit more than what I expected."

The man jumped up, excited, "Oh good! Good!" He walked over to Gary. "You have no idea how much that means coming from an aficionado such as yourself." He took a cigarette from his jacket pocket. "You mind if I smoke?" He lit up before Gary could answer.

"I don't mean any disrespect, but can you tell me why you're here? Why you *broke into* my apartment?"

"Please forgive me for that," the man said, sitting down again on the chair beside Gary's bed. "I watched your face during the screening. You looked a tad repulsed, as is common for first timers, but as it went on, you didn't. In fact, I'd say you looked downright thrilled. Am I right?"

Gary had no idea where this was heading, but "thrilled" isn't how he'd describe his thoughts watching the snuff film, regardless of how his face may have looked at the time. "Like I said, it wasn't what I had expected."

"Right, right... you figured you'd see a priest get stabbed or shot or hung, but you weren't expecting the work of art my boys and I created, were you?"

Playing along, worried this guy was about to snap, Gary said, "You could say that."

The man smiled. "You see Gary, not many people who come to see my films last very long. The older gentleman who was at today's screening with you? He had a heart attack a few minutes after he arrived at his son's house in Staten Island."

*Dear God,* Gary thought. These guys weren't taking any chances with anyone. He was still worried that he was about to be killed, until the man knelt before him, at which point Gary's concern turned to discomfort. He shifted and leaned away from the man thinking he might try to kiss him or something, but instead the man took his hands and held them firmly. They felt incredibly warm, but not sweaty like his were.

"Gary, I want you to work for me."

"What?" Gary said, trying to pull his hands away, but the man held on tightly.

"Are you deaf? I said I want you to work for me."

"I-I can't ... I'm not a killer!"

"No, no, no. I have people for that end of the job." The man looked to the corner of the room where an old-school editing machine sat. Gary's grandfather had given it to him when he was eight years old to help him make Super 8 movies. "You know how to make films, I assume?"

Gary's heart quickened. It had been more than a decade since he'd put his dream of filmmaking aside in favor of living like a responsible adult. Now it was nothing more than fodder for the occasional daydream about what could have been if his short film had lit the festival world on fire the way he had envisioned, rather than fizzle out with an audience award at a rinky-dink festival, and a few positive mentions for FX.

Instead of going to college, Gary spent the 10-Gs his parents had been saving since he was a kid to fulfill the dream that everyone told him was unattainable. He spent the money on FX alone and hired a pro with several feature films to his name. All told, it cost double that. And the guy was a huge douchebag who acted like the job was beneath him. Gary had banked on everything in the hope of...

Best case – securing a deal for a feature-length version of the short.

Worst case – simply gaining a minor foothold in the industry.

In the end, Gary was just another broke 20-something living in his parents' basement. And they weren't about to let him forget that. He was reminded every few years when he'd catch a trailer for the latest Jonas Marks film on TV. Marks' first short film swept the festivals the same year Gary's film screened. They had even developed a friendship that ended when Marks stopped returning his calls.

A few more opportunities had come and gone through the connections Gary had maintained within the local independent film community; false starts and sure things that fell apart for reasons beyond his control.

There was the producer, from Philly, who had stumbled upon Gary's short, and loved it. He offered to executive-produce a feature-length version, for a budget of 1.5 million, but only if Gary changed everything that made the film unique. Gary tried to accommodate the producer's demands, while "gently" pushing back against the man's more extreme, and in Gary's opinion, self-indulgent ideas. But the producer eventually lost interest and backed out of the project. To add insult to injury, he gave Gary a lecture about film being a collaborative project, and not looking a gift horse in the mouth.

Then, there was the German investor Gary had met at an industry networking event. They had hit it off over drinks and their love of extreme horror cinema, and when the man asked Gary about his next project, he pulled a premise out his ass for a low-budget shocker, shot in one location, with only two actors. At the time, Gary was still reeling from his experience with the Philly producer and had yet to consider his next move. The film he pitched to the German investor, about a young couple being stalked by their older selves, was based on themes that had been percolating in his mind for some time, but that he had never been able to pull together into a cohesive story until it rolled off his tongue that night. The investor was hooked from the start. It was perfect—a big idea masked by a small one. The film was going to be Gary's mainstream calling card as it was deeper than his usual ideas, while still containing a healthy dose of extreme violence that was relative to the plot this time and not gratuitous, which was a common critique of Gary's short. The investor suggested a $500.000 budget.

Due to their fast 'friendship,' Gary didn't insist on a contract, and after spending the better part of a year developing the project and shaping it into a filmable script, the investor ghosted him, and sent an email from his lawyer, claiming ownership over the script and threatening legal action should Gary attempt to use it for his own purposes.

Gary considered taking legal action against the investor, but with no contract, it was his word against that slimy, back-stabbing piece-of-shit's.

Once he was able to revisit the project without the wallop of PTSD that usually came with the memory of it, he reworked the story into a lean, mean script about rogue angels indulging in Earthly pleasures. The new script made it all the way to the top five in the running for the grand prize in the New York International Screenplay Competition, but ultimately took second place. The reward was a free workshop with a well-known, working screenwriter whose resume translated to: *Horror films are beneath me*. No thanks.

With each opportunity, Gary allowed himself to believe that it was finally going to happen this time. He dished out figurative 'I told you so's' to all the people in his life who had told him, in so many words, to stop wasting his time on this Hollywood pipe dream, to get a real job. And with each failure, the weight of their judgement grew heavier.

As if reading Gary's mind, the man said, "Look at it as a chance to be a filmmaker again."

"How'd you know about that?" asked Gary.

"Like I said at the screening: we know more about you than you think. And I don't mean that to sound as ominous as it might come across. It's just that this line of work requires the utmost vigilance when it comes to vetting potential employees. I'm sure you understand."

Gary thought for a moment. "No offense," he said, "but as far as redeeming myself as a filmmaker, snuff films aren't exactly the kind of thing you wanna go around bragging about."

"I do," the man smiled. "What I meant was that you can use the money you make to finance your own film."

Part of the occasional daydream was that Gary would somehow scrounge up enough cash to give it another go at making a film.

Scenarios on how he'd acquire that cash ranged from a surprise inheritance from some long-lost relative, who didn't exist, to winning the lottery. But here was a real opportunity, right in front of him.

The man gave Gary a deep, pleading look, waiting for a response.

After an eternal minute, Gary said, half disappointed, "I have a decent job. And I really don't want to get involved with this stuff. You know what I'm saying?"

The man dropped Gary's hands, stood up, and pulled a roll of hundreds from his pocket. He counted off too many for Gary to keep up with. "But does it pay you this much for one day's work?"

The man handed the bills to Gary. He counted them and his heart rate went even higher. Twenty-five hundred bucks. *Holy shit.*

The man began walking out of the room. "You hold onto that and sleep on it. I'll call you tomorrow. The day after, even. There's no rush."

As he left the apartment, Gary heard the man say, "Sweet dreams."

# 5
---

The offer consumed Gary's thoughts as he waited for his phone to ring. He jumped in excitement at every text alert or email chime like a smitten teenager.

Gary's refuge had been breached by the man with the creepy-cool charisma that was both strangely disarming and intimidating. As a result, the solace he often sought from his inner sanctum of signed horror movie posters and obscure memorabilia just wasn't cutting it.

Gary turned to the Sail Inn for comfort. The bartender was restocking the bar when he entered. This time the TV was tuned to some house-flipping show.

It had only been a few hours since his last visit.

The place was decorated with the same poor souls. The man at the bar who had been angling for a conversation earlier looked happy to see him.

Gary evaded the eager man's glance as he sat down at the bar and placed his credit card on the counter. He made sure to sit further away from the conversationalist this time.

The bartender approached Gary with a cordial smile on his face while wiping his hands with a towel.

"Same as before?" he asked.

Gary nodded. "But make the Jim Beam a double."

"Still having a bad day?" the bartender said when he returned with the drinks and placed them in front of Gary.

"Huh? Oh. Yeah," he said, "You would think..."

"Well... TGIF, I guess."

"It's Friday?" he asked, having genuinely forgotten what day it was.

The bartender shared a quizzical look with the conversationalist down the bar.

"Last time I checked," he said to Gary.

Gary nodded, and then slammed the shot and gulped down the entire glass of Jim Beam. He placed the empty glass down on the bar and scrunched his face in reaction to the kick of the booze. He took a moment to recover, and then knocked back half of the Guinness.

The bartender returned a sympathetic smile as he placed Gary's credit card next to the old-school cash register and went back to restocking the bar. At some point Gary heard one of the patrons ask, "Is there something else on?"

"Beats all the virus horseshit," the bartender said of the house-flipping show as he thumbed through channels. "We've become such pussies in this country that we're getting all bent out of shape over a tummy-ache."

"If it's even real," the barfly said.

Both men chuckled. "Amen to that," the bartender said. "I'm skeptical of anything I hear in the mainstream media."

"You and me both, brother," the barfly said, raising his glass in agreement. "You and me both."

For a moment, Gary questioned his dismissive stance on the matter as it aligned him with men of such *staggering intellect*. Not that he was some pinnacle of intelligence or anything, but he was definitely a few rungs above these low-brow contrarians.

"For the record, I only watch that show to get tips on fixing things around the house," the bartender added.

*Might wanna apply some of that to fixing up this place.* The bartender stopped on a show about historical mysteries. Some TV-ready historian/conspiracy-theorist spouting on about the Internet being a creation of the Devil.

"Of course, it is," the bartender quipped sarcastically. "Ain't this the same jag-off who used to go around in the '90s saying 'TV is the Devil'?"

"I don't know," replied the barfly. "Kinda makes you wonder, though."

The bartender looked over at Gary and made a face.

Gary forced a smile and then quickly broke eye-contact.

At the forefront of Gary's thoughts was the image of the man sitting in the chair beside his bed. It filled him with a feeling of help-lessness that reached deep down to his soul and left him with a raging kaleidoscope of butterflies.

*This is a guy who makes his living off murder. Who knows how involved with the actual killings he is or has been in the past? And he was in YOUR apartment... uninvited. What's a guy like that capable of?*

After a few more rounds of Jim Beam, Gary stopped obsessing over it and focused on taking measures to ensure it would never happen again.

"Will I see you again, today?" the bartender asked as Gary closed out his tab.

"Let's hope not," Gary replied with a straight face, and then he got up from his seat and walked out the door.

Gary used the advance the man had given him to buy new locks for all the doors and windows in his apartment.

He made a few impulse purchases from his wish list: tickets to the Goblin Show at the PlayStation Theater in Manhattan, a leather-bound book of lobby cards, and the original Italian poster for Fulci's *The Beyond,* signed by the man himself. Gary had his eye on that baby for a while.

From there Gary stumbled into an all-too-common fantasy of rubbing elbows with his favorite living filmmakers as they lavished praise on his work and treated him like a peer, and celebrity. Fast cars. Exotic locales. Beautiful women. All the shit he pretended to loathe whenever the subject of filmmaking came up in mixed company.

At some point, the fantasy shifted dark, the priest's gory death coming into the mix in creative ways, written and directed by Gary's own morbid curiosity and guilt. It kicked Gary off his cloud and got him stressing over the details.

Who were the victims in these films? The man had mentioned that the priest was convicted of molesting children. Assuming the other films were on par with the priest's, what had the other victims done to deserve such a sadistic end?

# 6

It took all day, but Gary felt a little more at ease once he changed the locks. His landlord would have something to say about it, but he'd cross that bridge when he came to it.

Now that he had reclaimed his sanctuary, Gary made a short list of his favorite films and plucked them from his collection. It would take a marathon to get his mind right. He'd open with a Pornhub grip-n-tug session, and then spend the rest of the weekend in self-appointed cinema therapy.

As hard as he tried, Gary couldn't sink into movie-watching mode. He was barely able to come from the grip-n-tug despite eight Pornhub windows. Even with his go-tos represented (Curvy Milf DP, Lesbian Strap-on, Gloryhole Wives) Gary struggled to finish. And when he finally did, the feeling was a resounding 'Meh.'

There was just too much to think about. Too much to over-analyze. Too much anxiety as he waited for the phone to ring, and from the compulsion to check his cell phone every five minutes.

Gary drifted through the weekend on autopilot, passively watching his favorite films while immersed in deep contemplation and doing his best to stave off jarring images of the priest, and the

Sawzall. He examined the man's offer from every possible angle, inside out, and upside down.

Gary had mixed emotions when he woke up Monday morning. Part of him was disappointed that the man had yet to call, and he wondered if he had somehow blown the deal. He sighed at the thought of going into the office as he sat on the edge of his bed, a tired, groggy husk, watching his resurrected movie career—and all the things he'd buy—fly away into the ether.

And there was something else, an instant regret that he wouldn't appease the adrenalized desire to leave his comfort-zone in the dust. It had been slowly festering in the pit of his belly for the latter half of the weekend. The thought of shooting snuff terrified him, yet also excited him in an almost sexual way.

At the same time, there was a sense of relief, a lessening of the pressure to commit.

Gary played the man's voice over and over in his head: *I'll call you tomorrow. The day after, even. There's no rush.*

At the office, the typical workaday malaise was replaced with prolonged blank stares and indifference to customer complaints about *As Seen on TV* products not working as their gullible asses had seen on TV. Bendis/Schlesinger was the company behind the more obscure *As Seen on TV* kitsch.

Gary wasn't checking his cell phone as much, but he still gave it a look several times an hour.

Every call birthed a round of excitement, then disappointment, which greatly affected his repertoire of practiced responses, and the exaggerated concerned facial expressions that went along with them.

"My 'Wrist-ahoop' Arm-Fat Terminator aggravated my old rotator cuff injury," one customer complained.

"That's too bad, ma'am," Gary replied, bored. "Maybe you should've read the fine print."

"I've been using the 'Give That Guy a Hand,' Head Massager for six months now and, not only have I not grown a single hair, now I've got a rash like nobody's business from the thing," said another. "And somebody wanna tell me why I've been on hold for like 20—"

"Blah. Blah. Blah," Gary shot back. "So, I'm assuming you want your money back?"

"You okay? You don't seem yourself today," said the likeable, 40-something divorcee in the cubicle to Gary's right, the one who lived with her mother and took pride in her extensive knowledge of every twist-and-turn of whatever vanilla TV series was popular.

Gary often wondered if he sounded like that when he gushed about his favorite horror films, broke down specific scenes, over-explained the subtext beneath them, and made long-winded fanboy dissertations about why the filmmakers he admired should be held in the same regard as Kubrick or Scorsese. Younger Gary might've felt self-conscious at the thought.

"Yeah. I was gonna say the same thing," commented the young man to to Gary's left.

Gary blew off their concern in a way that only made them more curious, and then he returned to the convoluted discourse inside his head.

He answered a few more calls and blew off a few more customer complaints before his boss, Dave Satterfield, appeared at the doorway of his cubicle and said, "Can I see you in my office?"

*Shit, shit, shit!* Gary thought as his boss walked away. The last thing he needed was a lecture from a 29-year-old kid who probably whacked off to movies like *The Boiler Room*. The way he felt right now, he'd end up saying something that would get him fired.

The phone rang and made Gary jump. He shot a glare at the thing and pursed his lips before snatching it from the receiver.

"Lemme guess," he snapped. "Whatever it is, doesn't work like it did on the infomercial?"

"Hello Gary," came a mellow, cocksure voice that Gary instantly recognized. "Catch you at a bad time?"

Gary froze. His heart raced. The man spoke in such a distinctive timbre that Gary could almost see his face as if it were hovering right there in front of him, pressing him for a response. And for a few passing seconds, Gary had nothing.

"Are you going to answer me, Gary, or are you just going to sit there, hang-jawed, with the phone glued to your ear while your boss waits for you outside his office?"

Gary whipped around and saw Dave Satterfield standing by his office doorway shooting daggers back at him. He flashed a nervous smile and gestured, *just a moment*, with his finger.

"That's right, Gary," said the voice on the other end of the phone. "Make him wait. You're dealing with things his Ivy League Education never prepared him for."

Heart still racing, Gary leaned forward and whispered into the phone. "How'd you get this number?"

"It's not that hard to find, Gary."

Gary hesitated. He heard a door slam, turned toward the sound, and saw that Dave Satterfield's office door was closed.

*Not good.*

A gang of curious eyes darted over the tops of cubicle walls. They looked away and ducked out of sight when Gary spotted them.

Gary leaned forward again and whispered into the phone. "This isn't the place to talk about this."

"I couldn't agree with you more, Gary," the man replied. "How 'bout lunch?"

# 7

———

"You seemed a little edgy on the phone earlier," the man remarked, a devilish smile peeking out from behind his beard. "Trouble at work?"

"How can you be so nonchalant about it?" Gary said, looking around, keeping his voice low.

"About what?"

"Come on. You know what I mean."

They sat across from each other at an outdoor café populated by stuffy, artistic types who probably thumbed their noses at genre films that weren't directed by Hitchcock or Kubrick. The hustle and bustle of mid-town Manhattan was lighter than usual, and every sixth person or so was wearing a surgical mask, or some artful variant. There was a high-brow hipster seated two tables away wearing a homemade cloth mask with the symbol for Pi printed on the mouth.

"About the virus?" the man joked, shifting a rather emotionless gaze from the hipster over to Gary, who wasn't sure how to respond.

Was this the man's way of telling Gary that personal questions were off limits or was he simply fucking around? And, if he *was* fucking around, then what kind of shriveled, blackened, putrefied pit of a heart must this guy have to make light of his occupation?

It had been an unusually warm February, and today was no differ-ent. The early afternoon sun gave Gary his first real look at the man's face, which was mostly eyes hovering over a bushy, Van Dyke-style beard. They were a pale shade of blue, cold and vacant, and set within a narrow face that exuded a sly confidence.

The man took a sip from his coffee and leaned back in his chair. Stroking his beard, he looked at Gary with amusement. "It's just a job, Gary," he said. "Nothing more. I suggest you adopt a similar attitude should you accept my offer. And, for the record, I hope you do."

Gary scrolled through potential responses in his head. There was so much he wanted to ask, but it was hard to concentrate.

"When I hadn't heard from you by this morning, I started to think that maybe you changed your mind," Gary said.

"I realize it's a big decision..." The man began.

Gary made a face. "That's putting it mildly."

"...so, I figured I'd give you the weekend."

Gary nodded, fast-scrolling thoughts until one of them jumped out in front.

"How'd you know my direct line at work?" he asked, genuinely baffled. "Or what I was doing when you called... or about my boss?"

The man hesitated, and then shot back, "Magic."

Gary side-eyed the man, waiting to be let off the hook. And when that didn't happen...

"Wait a minute," he said in disbelief. "You're... *serious*?"

"Of course not," the man scolded.

"I was about to say," Gary said, smiling in embarrassment.

"What were you 'about to say,' Gary?"

"Oh. Just that, you know..." Gary stammered, feeling put on the spot. "It figures that maybe this guy's off his rocker. No offense."

"None taken. I've been called much worse."

"How *did* you know all those things I mentioned?" Gary asked.

"A few minutes on the company directory. A cheap pair of binocu-lars. A few little white lies to gain access to the building next to your office. And *voila*."

Gary was uncomfortable. A short dispute between drivers flared up in the background. The two men sipped their coffee and took in the brief drama.

"Who the hell drives into Manhattan?" Gary said.

"Only the very rich, according to the Governor," replied the man.

"I wouldn't say those two fall into that category." One drove a Kia and the other a blue Honda Accord with a rusted, red driver-side door.

"This virus has got everyone on edge," Gary said.

"It's only going to get worse," the man said knowingly.

Gary perked up. He was anxious for someone that he looked up to either validate or discredit the virus so he could finally decide how he should feel about it. Maybe 'looked up to' was too strong an assessment of Gary's feelings toward the man. Rather, someone for whom he felt fearful veneration: awe and approbation, who seemed more knowledgeable than he was on the matter. The man possessed an air of otherworldly wisdom.

"Why? What have you heard?" Gary asked.

"Same as you," the man replied. "It's more of a feeling. Humanity's due for a game-changer, in some way, shape, or form. Maybe this is it."

"Oh," Gary said, slightly disappointed.

The man smiled and sipped his coffee. Afterward, he leaned forward, rested his forearms on the table, focused his large, pale, vacant eyes on Gary, and said, "So. Have you decided?"

Gary took deep, calming breaths and gave the question careful consideration. Eventually, he exhaled and then said, "A few things before I give you my answer."

"Okay."

"Regarding the victims..."

The man raised a hand. His expression shifted serious. "The talent," he corrected.

"Excuse me?"

"Not victims. *Talent.*"

"My apologies. The...*talent*," Gary said, handling the word with trepidation. "You mentioned that the priest was accused of child molestation. Have they all done something... committed some kind of crime? Or are these just innocent vict...talent?"

"That depends on how you define innocence," the man replied.

Gary's decision was predicated on the victims. As much as the adrenaline rush of crossing societal boundaries made him horny for the experience, the idea of contributing to outright murder, if that was indeed what was going on here, made him sick to his stomach. It was difficult for Gary to hide his annoyance with the man's vague response.

"Sure. People lie, cheat, and steal from each other every day," Gary said, maintaining a relatively quiet voice. "But in a civilized society, none of that stuff warrants death. And what about the kids? What could they have possibly done to deserve—"

"Some people believe that we are all born guilty of sin," the man said.

"Well. Those people need to pull their heads out of the bible and get a life." A few seconds passed. "You're not one of them. Are you?" Gary asked nervously.

"Would it matter if I was?"

Gary had to think about it.

"The world is a much more complex place than you know, Gary," the man said. "You play your cards right and maybe one day you'll come to understand that."

Gary wasn't sure what he meant. His concerns about the victims had not been addressed to his satisfaction.

"If it eases your mind, I can assure you that the talent have all earned their roles in their respective films," the man followed up, detecting Gary's disappointment.

"No kids," Gary said shortly after. "I don't even want to know about that side of it."

"Done."

"And no more spying on me or showing up at my place unannounced. I understand the need for caution, but you should know by now that I'm not some schmuck off the street who can't handle it. If I'm gonna do this, there's gotta be some level of trust. I mean... you can't expect me to put out quality work if I'm always looking over my shoulder... or under the bed... or in the closet."

The man didn't respond right away. His eyes were fixed on Gary, which led Gary to believe that maybe he had crossed a line. But then a smile took shape. Even the man's eyes were affected by it.

"Well said," the man said. "Trust is a hard thing to come by in this business. I will do my best to work on that. For the sake of the films."

Gary was pleasantly surprised.

"Anything else?"

"I was thinking that I'd like to work under a pseudonym," Gary said. "In the interest of caution, of course," he added, lest the man think him some pain-in-the-ass, artsy type.

"You do know these films have no credits, right?"

"Yeah," said Gary. "I meant what you and everyone else on set can call me."

The man smirked as if he was talking to a starry-eyed pipe-dreamer.

"Sure," he replied, and leaned forward. "Whatcha got for me?"

"Lee Revok," Gary said proudly. "Lee was a family nickname given to me when I was a kid, because I was the 'spitting image' of my uncle Lee. And Revok after a character in one of my favorite Cronenberg films."

"Scanners. Right?" the man uttered with confidence. "Michael Ironside's character."

Gary couldn't help but smile. "That's right," he said, delighted by the man's knowledge of horror cinema.

"Interesting film."

"*Great* film! Great actor, too. Criminally underrated. Have you seen—" Gary stopped himself. "Sorry. It doesn't take much to get me excited about movies."

"I can see that," the man said. "Is there anything else?"

Gary thought for a moment. "I think that's it," he finally said.

The man finished his coffee, placed his cup down on the table, and looked at his watch.

"You'll receive a text from me with the time and location of the first shoot sometime this afternoon," he said to Gary. "You'll respond 'Yes,' or 'No,' to the text. I'll only text one time for each job. If you don't respond within five minutes of receiving the text, I'll consider that a no, and move on to the next available operative."

"Understood," said Gary, trying to hide the fear-tinged excitement that bubbled inside him. "How many of these can I expect to do... in a month, let's say?"

"Three or four, on average."

Gary raised his eyebrows. *That's a lot of death.*

"There's no shortage of talent these days," the man said, grinning wryly.

"And each time it's twenty-five hundred, cash?"

"What I gave you to hold was only half."

Gary was caught off guard. He reacted as if jolted by electricity, and leaned forward and mouthed, "Five thousand dollars?"

"That's right," the man said.

Gary leaned back in his chair and did some refiguring in his head. A big, dumb smile formed on his face.

The man wiped the corners of his mouth with a napkin, and got up from the table. "One of these days," he said, "you and I will have to get together and talk movies. I think you'll find that our tastes are very similar."

Still smiling, Gary shook his head. "You're full of surprises, aren't you?" he said.

"Not really."

The man extended a hand to Gary, a friendlier smile than usual on his face. Gary shook the man's hand.

"Looking forward to working with you," the man said.

"Likewise."

As the man started to walk away, Gary remembered something he had forgotten to ask. "What do I call you, by the way?"

"You can call me Thirty-six," said the man without looking back.

*Thirty-six?*

Assuming it was a pseudonym, Gary tried to make sense of it as the man walked down the street. Maybe it was his age, although he looked closer to Forty-six. Maybe it was his favorite number for no other reason than he liked the sound of it. Could've been anything.

Eventually, the steady flow of human traffic swallowed the man whole.

# 8

Gary was so busy reflecting on his lunch meeting that he didn't even remember the walk back to work.

The sight of 2105 Crescent Boulevard across the street brought with it new concerns. Bendis/Schlesinger lived on the 12<sup>th</sup> floor of the building. Gary had left Dave Satterfield hanging when he hurried off to lunch, and now he was likely looking at a write-up for insubordination in addition to a long-winded reprimand.

He could just tell Dave to fuck off, and be done with Customer Service. Three-to-four shoots a month at five Gs a pop. That's one hundred eighty to two hundred forty grand a year. More than four times his salary.

But Gary didn't want to burn that bridge. What if he couldn't hack it shooting snuff films?

As he stood on the corner waiting for the light to change, Gary fixated on the building to the left of 2105, some old apartment building converted into a Lowe's Hotel. That's where Thirty-six would've been watching with his binoculars.

There were no windows on the side of the Lowe's that faced Gary's building. Plastered across two thirds of the flat concrete façade was a billboard for some obnoxious romantic comedy starring that annoying ingénue whose name no one could pronounce. Gary had seen the thing through the window a million times while languishing at his desk. Before that it was an ad for Axe Body Spray, and before that, an ad for Captain Morgan Rum.

The traffic light had changed some time ago. The cluster of mostly masked office-jockeys who waited with Gary had already crossed, leaving him there alone.

Gary crossed, eyes darting back-and-forth between the billboard and the 12th floor window of his building.

"There you are," Dave Satterfield groaned when Gary walked into his office and closed the door. He didn't even bother to say goodbye to whomever he had been speaking with on the phone before hanging up and focusing a sudden explosion of ire on Gary. "You know, you're lucky I don't—"

"I need to use some of my vacation days for a family emergency," Gary interrupted, stomping all over Satterfield's rebuke. He had tapped into the overflowing well of anxiety to give his request a weighty authenticity. "I'm sorry for the short notice, but it came on suddenly."

Dave's eyes lingered on Gary, narrowing as he leaned far back in his chair and crossed his arms. Satterfield wasn't enough of a dick to kick a man while he was down, so his anger would have to be suppressed for now. It was clear that he still had much to say.

"I'm sorry to hear," Dave said in a tone of practiced concern. "I hope it isn't anything serious."

"It's about as serious as it gets, unfortunately," Gary said. "I've known about it since Friday, but then I got a call today that changed everything. That's why I rushed out of here. My apologies for that, by the way."

Dave nodded and appeared to think it over. "Why didn't you just tell me?" he said in a much more sympathetic tone.

"I've just had so much on my mind for the past few days."

"Well, look. Take as much time as you need," Dave offered, which really meant *Take up to your remaining eight vacation days, and no more.*

"Thanks for understanding," Gary said.

"I know it might not seem like it right now, but you'll get through this."

"Thanks," Gary responded as he motioned for the door.

"When my father died," Dave continued, "I thought I would never get over—"

But Gary was already out the door.

He spent the train ride home answering texts from his coworkers, who expressed their sympathy regarding his 'family emergency,' while fishing for more information on the subject. They did everything short of coming out and asking him if it had anything to do with the virus. Gary worried that the lengthy responses he came up with to bolster the lie might somehow clog up his cell phone and block Thirty-Six's text, even though cell phones don't work like that.

Gary's plan for the night was a prolonged grip-n-tug, followed by some time re-acquainting himself with the filmmaking techniques that were to be his calling card when he made it big as a director, and reading up on the latest in filmmaking cameras and equipment. In fact, he couldn't wait. While he wasn't sure how much leeway he'd have with the snuff films, he'd certainly try to stand out from the other directors.

Then he began wondering about those very individuals. Who were they? Were they failed dreamers turned work-a-day stiffs like him, or some whole new species of twisted auteur?

Thirty-Six's text came as Gary exited the train.

**February 28$^{th}$ @6am**
**1347 Luxemburg (The old YMCA Building)**
**Show up a half hr early. A few things to discuss**
**Do you accept? Y/N**

GARY'S first thought as he walked along the train platform and up the steps was the YMCA where he went to summer camp as a kid.

He answered 'Y' letting his thumb hover over the 'Send' button for a while before pressing it.

The 28$^{\text{th}}$ was tomorrow. He checked the date on his phone to make sure.

# 9

"Hi. I'm Gar—Lee. Lee Revok," Gary said as he extended his hand toward the heavily tattooed Hispanic man who answered the door of old YMCA on Luxemburg. The same guy from the Stor-Right screening.

Instead of reciprocating, the man glanced down at Gary's outstretched arm, as if to assess it as a threat, and said, "Good for you."

He stuck his head out the door and looked both ways before letting Gary in.

Inside, the same Jamaican fellow from the Stor-Right screening leaned against the wall, typing on his phone. He looked up long enough to nod *hello* as the Hispanic man patted Gary down. Thankfully, he had left his .22 in the car.

The place was much the same as he remembered from childhood, save for the boarded-up windows, the improvised living quarters made of old clothing and linens, the clusters of cigarette butts, used syringes, and the layers upon layers of graffiti.

The Hispanic man led Gary down the main hallway and through a large gymnasium, where he remembered playing basketball. The glassless backboard was still mounted to the wall on one side.

"I used to go to summer camp here back when the dinosaurs walked the Earth," Gary said, attempting to lighten the mood.

"I don't care," the Hispanic man said.

*I guess we're not doing small talk.*

They walked toward a door on the other side of the room. 'Locker room/Showers' was barely visible above the door.

A 10'x 10' cage meant for dogs had been set up in the middle of the open shower area. Thirty-Six was standing by the entrance of the thing speaking with a man wearing the same get-up as the guys who mutilated the priest. Gary was something resembling starstruck.

Thirty-Six excused himself when Gary entered the room looking like a lost tourist and walked over to greet him. He nodded to the Hispanic man who stood holding the door open. The man nodded back and let the door close.

"Not much of a conversationalist, that one," Gary said of the Hispanic man as he and Thirty-Six shook hands.

"You'll find that people value their anonymity in this line of work, *Mr. Revok*," said Thirty-six, leading Gary to a camera on a sturdy tripod. A hooded man in black was bent over it, fumbling with settings. He was dressed the same as the other one, down to the clear facemask.

"Well, that answers my next question," Gary said making eyes at the hooded, masked men.

"Assistants," Thirty-Six said.

"Same ones every time?"

"Usually. We like to keep the circle small."

A minor detail escaped Gary until now. Each of the assistants had a Glock 9 tucked into the back of their waistbands.

"Are they always armed?" he wondered aloud.

"Just a precaution," Thirty-Six assured him.

*Precaution against what?* Gary wanted to ask, but he kept his mouth shut out of fear of what the answer might be.

He looked around the room, his memory restoring it to its early-70s bluster.

The graffiti was more elaborate, like the artists had time to groove.

Underneath the colorful strokes, dirt-caked white tiles were chipped, broken, and raining dust that had settled in piles on the floor. Everything echoed.

"All set, sir," said the assistant by the camera, his voice muffled by the mask.

"Good," Thirty-Six said, tapping the assistant on the shoulder.

The assistant left the room through a back door.

Thirty-Six glanced over at the assistant working the lighting.

"A couple more minutes," the masked assistant said in a similarly muffled voice that sounded female to Gary.

Thirty-Six nodded and turned to Gary.

"While we're waiting, I want to go over a few things with you," he said.

"Okay."

He handed Gary a form on a clipboard to sign.

"What this?" Gary asked.

"Just a standard contract."

Gary pretended to peruse the contract. He was way too excited to care about the fine print. Thirty-Six handed him a pen and he signed the thing without hesitation.

"The main thing is to keep it simple," Thirty-six said. "Remember, you're not trying to impress some producer or studio-head here. All you have to worry about is pointing and shooting. You're free to go hand-held, if you'd like, but nothing flashy. It's what's going on in the cage that's important."

"What exactly is going on in there?"

"You'll see soon enough."

*Figures.*

"How will I know when to start filming?"

"You'll get a feel for that over time," Thirty-six said. "But for now, I'll let you know."

Gary nodded.

"Ever use one of these?" Thirty-Six asked, pointing to the camera, a BlackmagicDesign URSA Mini Pro.

"No, actually. But I've read about them."

Thirty-Six gave Gary a quick tutorial on operating the camera. Somewhere along the way, the lighting assistant yelled, "Ready!"

Thirty-Six nodded. "You ready to make your first *real* film?" he said.

Gary took a deep breath. "As ready as I'll ever be."

"Any questions before we get started?"

"No," he said. "I think I'm good."

"You *think*?"

"I'm good."

"That's more like it." Thirty-Six smiled and gave his shoulder an encouraging squeeze. "Okay," he called out. "Bring in the talent."

Gary was on pins-and-needles. He tensed at the sound of a voice from another room. It started as faint mumbling, but evolved into loud, pleading tones.

Just then, he felt a nudge in his side. It was Thirty-Six. "Now," he said, as if indicating that Gary should have begun recording.

"Oh shit," Gary said, distracted by the pleads from the next room and the horrors it conjured in his head. "Action!" he yelled, simultaneously pressing 'Record,' and swinging the camera around to face the back door.

The pleading tones were suddenly dampened. Seconds later, two assistants burst through the door escorting a third, naked man, arms cuffed behind his back, tears streaming down a face that was already swollen from crying. The ball-gag in his mouth was wet from a mixture of saliva and snot.

The naked man was the epitome of average, except for his penis, which was large and uncircumcised. He looked like he had been worked over just enough to break his spirit and take the fight out of him. His shoulders were slack, head hanging low, and no sense of shame or even embarrassment regarding his state of undress.

The average man's puffy, reddened eyes searched the room for an ally as the assistants led him toward the door of the cage. He looked straight into the camera, which gave Gary a chill.

There was a large padlock on the cage door. One assistant used a key to open it while the other one uncuffed the average man.

They shoved him inside. The man stumbled forward and turned around, looking right in Gary's direction. His eyes grew huge when he saw Thirty-Six standing next to him. The man motioned toward the still opened cage door.

"I wouldn't," came a voice from the assistant standing in the doorway of the cage, his hand resting on his pistol.

The average man heeded the advice and turned his attention to getting the ball-gag off his head.

The second assistant had left the room through the back door and returned moments later with a metal bucket full of something that he was careful not to spill as he carried it up to the cage door.

The assistant dowsed the average man with the contents of the bucket, which looked like milky water with chunks of skin and fat, possibly from a chicken.

The average man shrieked through the ball-gag and stiffened as the frigid liquid poured over him.

The assistant stepped back into the doorway. The other one left the room again.

The average man finally managed to remove the ball-gag. He kept Thirty-Six in his sights as he wiped the gunk from his face and mouth, hurried up to the cage wall, and grabbed hold of the links.

"Please," he presented his case directly to Thirty-Six. "You don't have to do this! I'll go back! You hear me? I promise I'll go back!"

Gary glanced over at Thirty-Six, wondering if he should turn the camera on him.

Thirty-Six shook his head "No."

Suddenly, the sound of dogs barking stole everyone's attention. It sounded like several of them, their baritone barks suggesting large breeds... and they were coming closer.

The average man's eyes filled with terror.

The back door swung open, and the assistant entered holding a quartet of large dogs on rope-leashes. The masked man was forced to lean back and dig in his heels to counteract the dogs' disjointed pulling toward the first thing they saw: the cage and the naked man inside of it. They moved forward like a barking, growling blur of filthy, matted fur, and snarling muzzles full of sharp teeth snapping shut and flinging off twisty bands of saliva. Within the blur, Gary made out a German Shepherd, possibly a Rottweiler, and a duo of formidable mutts.

The average man turned a desperate expression on Thirty-Six.

"Goddammit! Are you listening to me?" he yelled. "I said you don't have to do this!"

When Thirty-Six didn't respond, the man's expression morphed from fear to anger, and he yelled again, this time in a language that Gary had never heard before.

Gary glanced at Thirty-Six, who seemed angry, like he understood and took offense to whatever the average man was saying.

The unintelligible threat was interrupted by the dogs entering the cage, barking, snarling, and shoving each other out of the way for first dibs. Their claws skittered on the tile floor as they charged, four sets of eyes locked in a predatory glare on the average man.

The assistant quickly slammed the cage door shut and replaced the padlock.

The average man ran to the far corner of the cage and attempted to climb the links, but the dogs were on him before his feet left the ground. He cried out as the first one sunk its teeth into the bulbous meat of his calf and yanked him downward. The others were all over him before he hit the floor, jockeying for position as they scratched and mauled his naked body.

He thrashed and swatted, doing his best to defend against thrusting muzzles, and teeth clamping down and puncturing his soft, pliable flesh, over and over. Their heads whipped savagely, working chunks loose, and tearing them away from his thighs, arms, and torso. Stubborn strands of skin stretched and snapped like distressed rubber, blood pouring from garish wounds they left behind. A chorus of deep primal growls and cries of human anguish worked in concert to create a disturbing cacophony of echoed noise.

The dogs released and reestablishing their vice-like hold as the man's defensive bucking and flailing obscured one area and exposed another. They bit down again, dug in their hind legs, and commenced a multi-direction tug-o-war with his body, smearing the floor with a thick coating of blackened blood which acted as a lubricant, preventing the man from establishing a base from which to resist their pulling or to attempt to stand. The dogs were sliding as well, but they refused to let go, the taste of blood amplifying their hunger and their determination.

Gary wanted to cover his ears and look away, but Thirty-Six was probably critiquing his performance. So instead, he closed his eyes and conjured up a random upbeat tune in his head—"*Don't Worry. Be Happy,*" by Bobby McFerrin, which he loathed—to drown out the horrible din as the dogs continued to make a mess of the average man.

But the song only made things worse when Gary opened his eyes.

At this point, the average man's struggle was sluggish and sedate as what remained of him was dragged across the tile floor like a giant, limp chew-toy, covered in red paint and missing significant chunks. His ribcage was fully visible on the left side, teased by a swatch of skin and muscle with ugly, flayed edges that flapped open and closed.

One of the dogs burrowed its snout into a large wound in the man's abdomen and pulled at the viscera inside until it protruded enough to be devoured with relative ease.

There was so much blood now that Gary could smell it. Its sweet musk was a facet of violence that he hadn't foreseen, and it made him nauseous.

The average man was curled into a ball with his arms over his head, barely conscious. He seemed mostly concerned with keeping the dogs away from his neck as they continued their merciless consumption of the rest of his body.

One of the dogs caught wind of his scrotum and flaccid penis and attacked the area with extreme ferocity. It was undeterred by the pressurized spray of blood that colored its face red when it bit down and yanked.

The average man came alive in a way that Gary didn't think he was still capable of. He shrieked in an unusually high pitch and convulsed involuntarily.

Gary's nausea was such that he couldn't hide it anymore. He slapped his hand over his mouth and, inspired by a sense of emergency that trumped his fear of a bad critique from Thirty-Six, turned and ran for the door, lurching violently and belching bile fumes into his clammy palm.


"I'M SORRY. I tried my best to fight it," Gary said as he stood with Thirty-Six in the old stairwell outside the gymnasium.

"Don't worry about it," Thirty-Six replied in a tone that, to Gary's delight, showed no signs of anger or disappointment. "First time's always the hardest."

Gary leaned against the wall next to an old, gunk-stained window, looking out at the empty YMCA parking lot through a broken pane. Rusted, wire-mesh security bars over the window cut the scene into diamond-shaped segments.

"Will this affect my pay?"

"Not at all," Thirty-Six said. "To be honest, I expected it."

Gary nodded, still dazed from the shoot, but feeling slightly less embarrassed.

"Speaking of which," Thirty-Six added, reaching into his blazer and pulling out a legal-sized envelope with L. Revok scribbled on the front. "For you... Mr. Revok," he smiled as he handed the envelope to Gary.

"Thanks," Gary said, and took the envelope and placed it in his back pocket. "I'll clean up the mess I made in there. I just need a few minutes to—"

"Nonsense," Thirty-Six scoffed. "You're a director now. A director doesn't concern himself with mopping up vomit. The assistants will take care of it. Your job's done for today."

"What happens now?"

"The editors will take it from here. You go on home. Kick your feet up. Have a beer. Takes a while to process your first shoot. I'll be in touch regarding the next one."

*The next one!* The words hit Gary like a kick to the groin and he half-wanted to tell Thirty-Six that he was out. But the money... and the adrenaline rush... and the opportunity to make a legit film...

Thirty-Six led Gary out into the gymnasium where he heard the assistants cleaning up and disassembling the cage in the next room. Crazy fucks were listening to ABBA as they worked. He didn't hear the dogs, which made him wonder what they had done with them. It'd probably be hard to place four big, mean-ass dogs with a taste for human flesh.

"You know your way out. Right?" Thirty-Six asked.

"Same way I came in?"

"Yes."

"By the way," Gary called out. "What did the guy in the cage say to you earlier? And what language was that? I've never heard anything like it before."

"That makes two of us," Thirty-Six replied. "I'll have the editors cut that part."

Gary didn't even bother with the usual facilitators (movies and porn) to distract his racing thoughts away from the horrors he had witnessed in the YMCA showers, and from the rush of adrenaline-laced anxiety that it produced. His mind was busy extrapolating every little nuance of the event in the interest of determining his guilt or innocence. So far, the verdict was still out.

The debate had been ongoing since he left the YMCA shoot, and by the early evening, Gary was dead-tired, and had a massive headache. Sleep seemed like the only escape.

When he closed his eyes the man in the cage was there waiting with his terrified expression upon first hearing the dogs, his eyes shutting with sudden animation when the dog bit down on his scrotum and penis.

When he dozed off, Gary was chased awake by a pulsating storm-cloud of toothy muzzles, growling and lunging at him. He could feel their hot breath on his face. This cycle repeated for hours, until by 8pm, he'd had enough.

And then came the text from Thirty-Six.

March 1<sup>st</sup> @6am
4902 S. Wescott
Do you accept? Y/N

"SHIT, that's the day after tomorrow," Gary whined and blew out some air.

Rather than add to his stress by over what might be in store, Gary quickly typed "Y" and hit "Send."

Now he had an upset stomach to match his throbbing head. And he was wide awake.

Gary lived in a decent part of town, and anyone would tell you it still wasn't a good idea to go walking around alone at night, but Gary wasn't concerned in the least. He didn't even think to grab a weapon on the way out.

The streets were unusually quiet. Or maybe it was just that Gary was so detached from his surroundings that he couldn't hear a thing. He walked for hours with no real purpose or destination. Apparently, the usual night-time riff raff was on sabbatical. He wondered if the Gatekeepers had anything to do with that. Their recruitment flyers were everywhere.

Gary eventually found himself standing at the main entrance to Flushing Meadows Park, where homeless people and tweakers lurked after the sun went down. Not exactly the place to be at 12:27 am. A voice from behind reminded Gary of that fact.

"Aye, man. Didn't your mom ever tell you it ain't safe out here?"

Gary turned slowly, more confused than scared, and locked eyes with the owner of the voice—a gaunt tweaker brandishing a switch-blade in a shaky grasp. The young man's face was oddly stretched, like there was too much space between his nose and mouth, and his eyes were seriously bugged out.

"That's right," said the tweaker, as if to verify that this was, in fact, a robbery. "Now gimme your money and your cell phone, bitch."

Normally Gary would have run. He might have pulled his .22 if he had it on him, but he always doubted that he'd have the wherewithal to actually pull the trigger in a real situation.

The difference tonight was that the YMCA shoot had also left him feeling strangely empowered. His proximity to violent death, and the impression of control over it, was like winning a stare-down with the grim-reaper and flipping him off, to boot. No random tweaker could come close to that.

Gary gave the tweaker a lazy once-over that concluded with a protracted gaze into the young man's bug-eyes. This appeared to make the man nervous.

The tweaker looked around as if expecting to find the police or maybe a camera-crew standing behind him. Afterward, he lifted the knife higher, summoning his most threatening expression in case his would-be victim hadn't realized how sharp and stabby it was.

"You think I won't use this on you?" he warned Gary.

Gary's deadpan expression shifted. The corners of his mouth slowly lifted into a smile. He started to laugh. It began as a wheezing chuckle, graduating into full-on belly laughter.

The tweaker lowered the knife and backed away, looking as if Gary's reaction was the last thing he expected.

Gary pointed at the young man and laughed even harder.

The tweaker turned and ran away as fast as his skinny legs would carry him.

# 10

## ONE MONTH LATER

"Looks like somebody's movin' up in the world," Jake the bartender said to Gary as he refreshed his bourbon.

He was eyeing Gary's right arm.

"The watch," Jake said. "That's a Sandoz. Right?"

Hell if Gary knew what it was. He just liked the way it looked. Same with his upgraded wardrobe, which made him look like a Luxury Car Salesman with Mafia ties.

"Yeah," he quickly replied, looking around to see who had heard him. Then, not too subtly, he slid the sleeve of his shirt down over the sterling-silver timepiece.

"Those things cost a pretty penny, is all I'm sayin.'"

"Yeah," Gary repeated, half-present.

In the four weeks since he first stumbled into the Sail Inn, the place had gone from a convenient watering hole to his home away from home, and a necessary facet of the post-shoot come-down, even in the midst of the "stay-at-home" mandate issued by the governor.

Gary felt more cautious about Hyper VG due to all the horror stories that had been in heavy rotation on every news outlet on the planet—the countless videos of folks searching frantically for the nearest public restroom or sprinting toward a secluded spot with their hands clamped over their mouths or clutching their asses, or the domino effect of sudden projectile vomit. He had even made a mental note to purchase a mask, but never actually got around to it.

Jake knew where to place the napkin on the bar when Gary walked in the door, and he knew when to stop prying. He was more interested in the television anyway, where a pair of local News Anchors were discussing the current state of the virus. In New York, all non-essential businesses were closed. Other states were expected to follow suit. California had gone as far as to put the entire state on lockdown. According to the experts, it was only going to get worse.

Gary was on a first-name basis with all the regulars now. There was Gus Ryerson, who sat in the corner reading the Daily News, and Mark DiBenedetto, the barfly/conversationalist, who still angled for interaction with Gary that went beyond surface niceties. And, of course, Jake, who kept the bar open, on the down-low, despite the Governor's mandate. None of them wore masks. As they were all essentially breaking the law, an unspoken bond as rebels of the mandate had developed between them. Gary was 'the quiet one' who maintained some semblance of social distancing, and who refrained from the generally misinformed discussions that occasionally broke out, usually in response to something said on the news. His mind was otherwise occupied.

With four films under his belt, Gary had reached some level of acceptance of the grim subject matter and of his role in the production. He gave them titles in his head. The YMCA shoot was *Eaten Alive*. Then *Burning Man*. Then *Pin Cushion*. And finally, *Skin Deep*, the worst one by far. He caught one of the assistants puking in an alley after that shoot, unaware that Gary had seen his face when he slid up the clear mask to vomit. He was just a kid, for Christ's sake. Couldn't have been more than twenty-five.

Gary was haunted by unpleasant memories from each shoot. Aside from the time he awoke to a skinless man, in flames, screaming in pain as he slammed into the walls of his bedroom, Gary was able to look past them and see the opportunities that lie ahead.

He had developed a fondness for Thirty-Six, whose creepy-cool charisma he sought to emulate. He put aside the red flags pertaining to Thirty-Six's boundary-crossing surveillance tactics, the weird little things that didn't add up, all the secrecy regarding his superiors... and his dismissive attitude toward the virus, which, these days usually came with a lack of intellectual prowess.

On his last shoot, Gary felt comfortable enough to give slight direction to Thirty-Six's goons. He even began to visualize how he would have set up shots had this been his own film.

Perhaps this was the spark that he hoped would reinvigorate his passion for filmmaking. He ventured further, imagining himself back in the director's chair, helming his masterpiece, and showing those assholes at the Brooklyn Horror Film Festival that they had over-looked a true auteur.

Gary shifted on his stool and smiled at the symbolic flames simmering under his ass.

"I've survived far worse than Hyper VG," Thirty-Six said when Gary broached the subject of the virus at the last shoot. He delivered the response with such confidence that Gary believed that maybe he was somehow immune.

On the TV, a 'BREAKING-NEWS' story cut into the normal programming. Some kind of police activity outside of what looked like a church.

Gary squinted to read the headline at the bottom of the screen.

'VIGILANTE GROUP EXPOSES MAJOR DRUG RING RUN OUT OF THE SATANIC CHURCH'

It was a chaotic scene. A small squadron of S.W.A.T-like Gate-keepers soldiers congregated behind yellow police tape, arguing with masked police officers charged with keeping the crowd at bay as another pair of officers escorted a member of the drug ring out through the front doors of the church in handcuffs.

It was the assistant from the *Skin Deep* shoot whose face Gary had seen.

# 11

After finishing his drink, Gary left the Sail Inn and took his time walking back to his apartment. There were even fewer people in the streets, although the few he saw, jogging, pushing strollers through the park, were all wearing masks. He passed the bodega near his place and was surprised to find it open. Inside, the shelves were bare. He picked up the last two frozen dinners and one of three remaining gallon jugs of Poland Spring Water.

"You come late," the jolly, Hispanic septuagenarian behind the register remarked, the lower half of his face hidden behind a black cloth mask.

"Yeah," said Gary, barely present. "Work."

"No mask?"

Gary felt slightly embarrassed. He'd been ignoring the dirty looks from people he passed on the street, but this was the first time someone had called him out on it.

*Who are you to talk? You're not even supposed to be open,* Gary thought. But he ultimately chose a more diplomatic response, "Well," he said, "I've been meaning to get one, but everybody's sold out."

"I order some last week," the cashier said. "I put one aside for you."

"Thanks," Gary said, caught off guard by the man's generosity.

"Hope you no looking for toilet paper? They clean me out."

According to various news reports, toilet paper had become the official virus panic item.

"Thanks. But I'm good," Gary said.

"They say the virus make the... *diarrhea come*?" the cashier said while pantomiming the imagined event.

"Like a stomach virus on steroids, supposedly."

The cashier made a disagreeable face as he loaded Gary's items into a brown paper bag. "No thank you."

"No thank you is right," Gary said, paying and grabbing the bag.

"You come early next time," the cashier called out as he walked out the store. "I put some toilet paper aside for you, too."

Gary thought that was nice of the man, who, in the nine years that he'd been frequenting the bodega, usually for odds and ends and the occasional frozen meal between trips to the real supermarket, he'd hardly ever spoken to outside of small talk.

Soon Gary was back to obsessing over the breaking news item about the drug bust at the Satanic Church.

The young assistant's involvement, that he was part of a Satanic Church, intrigued Gary. He knew all about the Satanic Temple in Massachusetts and the Church of Satan which had started out in California before relocating to Manhattan, and then to Poughkeepsie after their founder's death. He also understood one as being more of a political organization and the other as an atheistic, hedonist group. Something about the wording on the newscast's scroll line made the group the assistant was involved with sound altogether different. And he remembered a line from a book he had read about Satanists written by a law enforcement official back in the 80s: *"However, 'real' Satanists aren't the spooky figures you see in films and pictured on heavy metal album covers. There exists a group identified as Satanists who, more-or-less, operate similar to the mob, just like an organized crime operation."*

After tossing one of the frozen, steak-and-potato dinners into the microwave, Gary booted up his laptop and opened a search engine. He typed SATANIC CHURCH NYC and was taken to a couple of death metal band links, one for the Satanic Temple, then finally one titled *The Official Website of the New York City Satanic Church.*

He followed the link to an ominous site. It was dark, but readable, not like most of the horror film sites he frequented with their amateurish designs, counterintuitive layouts, and clip-art navigation that suggested "cheap thrills." There was a rawness in this site's sparsity. There were no links for service times, no statement of beliefs, nothing he had seen on similar sites. There was, however, a location and a box to contact them via email.

He decided to look up the address.

The group appeared to meet in a small basement on Grand Street on the Lower East Side of Manhattan, close to a park and synagogue. When he zoomed in, the address from the website became clear on an ordinary looking apartment building, making the group even more mysterious. Perhaps they didn't want to draw attention to themselves being so close to a Jewish place of worship? Or perhaps they were another group who used Satanic rituals and imagery as an excuse to host orgies or drug parties?

Either way, Gary decided to take a ride and check the place out. He was surprised he had never heard of the group and wondered if anyone would even be there considering the drug-related accusations against them and, not to mention, the mandate. He'd seen the stories on the news about churches defying the mandate because they were "protected by God," and "duty-bound to carry on the gospel," and he figured if any church would be among that group, it would be the one that aligned itself with the Devil.

The steak in the frozen dinner reminded Gary of the hot lunch he was served in elementary school. The so-called *Salisbury Steak* always had a "pre-made" flavor, but he found the taste comforting. He even had a flash of nostalgia as he finished the meal, thinking of the time in third grade when he had traded his homemade lunch (a ham-and-Swiss sandwich) to Bobby Fisher for his Salisbury Steak from the kitchen. His mother would've killed him if she knew he preferred cheap frozen junk over her own prepared lunches, so he always kept that little secret to himself.

Gary stopped at the CTown Supermarket a few blocks from his place to look for a mask. The clerk directed him to the Health & Beauty Aisle where there was only one mask left: a black, cloth thing with a pair of juicy, red, puckered lips on the front. He searched the area several times, hoping to find another, one more his style.

Nothing.

Gary blew out some air, grabbed the mask, and made his way to the register.

He took the FDR Drive south to the Houston Street exit and then tapped the GPS app on his phone. Normally traffic would have been a bitch considering it was just before rush hour, but with fewer cars on the road, thanks to the virus, he found himself on Grand Street within fifteen minutes. He had passed the Landmark Sunshine Theater on E. Houston, at least, what used to be the Sunshine (as they called it). It had closed in 2018 and was slowly being taken down, piece-by-piece.

He had seen countless midnight movies there, including most of his favorites. He had also seen the first feature film by his nemesis, Jonas Marks there, and hated to admit that it was pretty damn good.

The Synagogue was an old but well-kept structure, and it let Gary know he was in the right area before the GPS mentioned that his destination was on the left. The church he had seen on the news was actually a Synagogue, but aside from different religious symbols, he'd never known the difference. He pulled over next to a busy-looking park and made his way to the front of 557A Grand Street on foot. It turned out the apartment was adjacent to a Chinese Restaurant that didn't show up on Google maps, making Gary wonder just how often the site was updated.

*This is The Satanic Church?* he thought as he went down a small flight of stairs to a basement apartment. On the wall next to the door at the bottom of the steps was a bell with a sign housing the initials SCNYC printed in old English-styled lettering. Gary wasn't sure what he would say as the door bounced closer, his curiosity in cahoots with his over-active imagination getting the best of him.

Gary put on his mask and took a moment to compose himself before he rang the bell. He was so preoccupied with the place that he had forgotten about the puckered lips on the face of his mask.

As he stood there waiting he wondered, for a fleeting moment, if he should fear for his safety. *Don't be silly*, he thought. It's not like a bunch of hooded cultists were going to open the door and pull him into a candle-lit room full of animal skulls and out-of-shape, middle-aged nudists...

After ringing a fourth time he decided no one was in, that his visit was a waste of time. Perhaps he should've just sent a message through their website, or maybe should've attempted further internet research. But as he turned to walk back up the stairs, he heard the door to the basement apartment creak open like in an old Hammer Horror film with haunted mansions and pale witchy redheads who were eager to disrobe. He wondered if it was a put-on or if the new-looking door actually needed to be oiled.

"May I help you?"

Gary turned back around and saw a man in a dark-colored suit looking out through the slightly opened door.

"Oh, hi," he said. "Sorry to bother you, but I was wondering if you had any information on your establishment? Any pamphlets or anything—"

"Nice mask."

The comment caught Gary off-guard, "Oh. Yeah," he chuckled nervously. "It was the only one left."

"What do you want here, Gary?"

Gary felt the hairs on the back of his neck stand at attention. And when the man stepped out from behind the door, he realized who it was.

"Not getting enough work from Thirty-Six, *Gary?* Or is it *Lee?*"

It was the Hispanic man who had let him into the YMCA building on the shoot he'd dubbed *Eaten Alive*. He flashed a friendly smile, thinking that the man would reciprocate given their familiarity with each other. Instead, he got the most sardonic, resting-bitch-face he had ever laid eyes on.

"So. What do they call you?" Gary asked, thinking that the ice had been broken between them.

"They call me the man with no name," he said.

Gary's face lit up.

"You mean like from the Leone films?" he said, suddenly excited.

The Hispanic man stared blankly.

"No. As in: *Don't ask.*"

"Oh," Gary said, feeling slighted.

*Maybe it was wrong to come here*, he thought. Had he broken some kind of unwritten rule, uncovered something, or seen something he wasn't supposed to?

"I saw this place mentioned on the news and decided to check it out," Gary said, his mouth suddenly dry.

The Hispanic man rolled his eyes. "So, you think this is a drug operation, do you? Well, it's not. And the pendejo who was caught with that shit will be put away for a long time. The police searched the place and saw his actions weren't a part of what we do here."

Gary didn't know what to say. He wished he had just contacted this place through their website, but now it was too late. He wondered if the Hispanic man would tell Thirty-Six he was here snooping around, or if Thirty-Six even knew about this place or that his doorman was a member.

Of course, he did. Thirty-Six knew *everything.*

"Sorry. Just wanted to check the place out. I didn't mean to intrude."

The Hispanic man opened the door. "Then check it out."

*You're not gonna put on a mask?* Gary thought about asking.

He tried to keep his calm as he entered the surprisingly well-lit vestibule while, in the back of his mind a dozen scenarios played out, each one ending in his violent death as punishment for sticking his nose where it didn't belong.

"Have a look around. I'll be right here."

Gary cautiously stepped through a curtained doorway. It led to a wide room that was a converted studio, or a two-room apartment. There was no altar, but a pentagram hung on the far wall with several seats facing it, like a small church. There were candles, none lit, and he didn't see any skulls, inverted crosses, or out-of-shape naked folks, nothing usually pictured in the horror films he grew up on. He counted fifteen seats and knew the place couldn't possibly be seeking to recruit, hence their quiet website. He wanted to ask the Hispanic man why they even had a website or an online contact form but decided not to. There was a second small room, but Gary just wanted to get out after having his curiosity partially sated.

On second glance, he realized that the pentagram on the wall wasn't inverted, which he had read somewhere was more a mark of witchcraft than Satanism.

"Nice set up," Gary said as he came back into the vestibule.

"Compared to what?" the Hispanic man asked with a stone-cold grin on his face.

"Compared to the Satanic Temple. I found that place a bit too showy."

"We're a different organization than they are."

His interest piqued, Gary wanted to ask how, but he kept quiet. He figured that if the man was going to reveal anything else, he would do it on his own. But after a silence, the man said nothing.

Gary thanked him and made his way up the stairs. When he got to the top step, he looked back down and saw the Hispanic man watching him as he slowly closed the door.

*What the fuck was that all about?* Gary thought as he made his way back to his car.

He expected Thirty-Six to call with a warning to stay away from the Satanic Church, but his phone remained silent during the drive back to Queens.

When he arrived home, Gary clicked on TCM and tried to relax to an old Spaghetti Western starring Lee Van Cleef, but he couldn't get the Hispanic man or the weird little church out of his mind. A block of commercials threw more cold water on his escapism attempt. He glanced around for the remote but didn't see it. He was too lazy to search the cushions, so he sat there stone-faced, looking past the screaming pitchmen and annoying jingles on the screen. A news brief came next. Of course, it was about the virus. Then reruns of The Jeffersons at 11 and 11:30. George and Wheezy, and...

A familiar face jumped out at Gary from the montage of characters and catchphrases, a reoccurring character who looked like he could've been the Hispanic man's Gamma-irradiated older brother. Hugo was his name.

*Handsome Hugo,* Gary chuckled in his head. It was the perfect nickname for the Hispanic man.

When the Western ended, he turned on the local news. Crammed between the endless updates and stories about the virus, he saw a repeat of the drug-bust footage he had seen in the bar earlier that afternoon. It gave him an idea.

Gary opened the Daily News website on his phone and searched the local crime reports.

# 12

---

Gary arrived at the 9<sup>th</sup> Precinct on E. 5<sup>th</sup> Street in lower Manhattan at 9:17 p.m. He was surprised how easily his bail money was accepted to release Daniel Varick from his holding cell, and even more surprised how low the fee was. He had brought $7,000.00 but didn't need a quarter as much. They had asked how he knew Mr. Varick, and he said they used to work at a film company together.

Gary hoped Daniel would simply accept that someone had bailed him out, and that he'd go along with whatever the policeman told or asked him. Or maybe Daniel felt he was safer in jail, thinking Handsome Hugo would have him killed the moment he walked outside.

He sat nervously in the waiting area, which was strangely barren, save for a chewed-looking man reading an outdated Entertainment Weekly, and an older woman who never blinked her eyes. Both were wearing standard, paper masks.

Gary doubled back to the chewed man, struck by something that had taken a while to reach him. On the cover of the Entertainment Weekly, beneath the Headline, *One to watch!* was a photo of Jonas Marks giving a thumbs up, a smile on his face that said, *I'm sittin' on top of the world, bitches!*

Gary chortled and dropped his chin to his chest. *Fucking figures*, he thought, shaking his head. Then he lost himself in speculation that his wild ride through the muck beneath the underbelly of cinema was, on some level, comparable to Jonas Marks' experience in mainstream Hollywood.

The sight of Daniel walking into the lobby put a hard-stop to Gary's envious conjecture. He was wearing the same type of paper mask as the chewed man and the unblinking woman, which Gary later learned were issued by the precinct staff to prisoners and visitors who didn't have one.

Daniel spotted Gary and walked over. He could see from the boy's eyes that he was smiling, which Gary figured was his reaction to gaining his freedom, until he offered his hand and said, "Love the mask."

Gary winced internally, having forgotten about the puckered lips on the front of the mask.

They shook hands and Gary started to explain the mask, but then he changed his mind and just said, "Nice to see you, Daniel."

"Not as nice as it is to see *you*," Daniel said, enthusiastic. "And it's Danny."

"Nice to see you, *Danny*," Gary corrected. "You ready?"

"Shit yes!"

～

"So. Whaddayou got some kinda safe-house set up?" asked a cautiously optimistic Danny as they drove back to Queens. He had the window down and was taking in the scenery with a new appreciation.

"Safe house?" Gary asked, like it was the first time he'd ever heard the term.

"Hey, look," Danny said, "I told the other dude that I wasn't agreeing to anything unless you guys can guarantee my safety."

"The hell are you talking about?"

Danny stared at Gary in disbelief, turning white. He slid further away and, as if he didn't want to know the answer, asked, "You're not with the Gatekeepers?"

"No, Why would you assume that?" Gary replied.

"I don't know. I thought maybe you were undercover. He doesn't usually hire guys like you."

"Guys like me?"

Danny hesitated, then reluctantly offered, "You kinda come off like a square. No offense."

Gary was mildly heartbroken, but now wasn't the time to dwell on it. If Danny's assertion had any merit, it meant that the Gatekeepers had some kind of interest in the church, or in Thirty-Six's cinematic endeavors, or in all the above. They were so interested, in fact, they were still pursuing said interest during a global fucking pandemic. And here he was right smack in the middle of it.

Gary spent the next few minutes convincing Danny that he hadn't come to collect him on Thirty-Six's behalf.

Word around the jail was that officials were considering releasing all the non-violent prisoners in a few days to slow the spread of the virus, which was tearing through the prison-system quicker than a virulent cluster of STDs through a crowd of spring-breaking coeds. As such, it seemed even more suspicious to Danny that someone was willing to drop $1,750.00 to bail out someone they hardly knew. Gary reassured him that he simply wanted to know more about Thirty-Six and the organization.

"What did the Gatekeepers want to know?" Gary asked.

"They kept talking about redemption and trying to get me to snitch on Thirty-Six. Said that they've been watching him for a long time and that they knew everything. 'So, whaddayou need me for?' I said. Then the guy asks me if I believe in hell. 'In the traditional sense,' he goes, 'fire and brimstone, eternal suffering, all that.' I mean, what the fuck? I think he was like their lawyer or something cause he was wearing a suit-and-tie. I never seen one of them in anything other than their usual S.W.A.T ninja getup."

For a while they drove in silence. Gary was troubled by the Gatekeepers' involvement, while Danny looked out the window like a coked-out housefly.

"*Do you* believe in hell?" Gary asked, breaking the silence.

Danny gave him a look. "I'll put it to you this way...I didn't before I met Thirty-Six."

Gary felt a chill run down his spine. He tightened his grip on the wheel and focused on the road.

Danny went on to reveal that, until his arrest, no one knew he dealt dope—let alone mainly to high school students—and he was sure they'd be coming after him if they weren't already.

*I'm pretty sure Thirty-Six knows,* Gary thought as Danny rambled on, looking out the back and side windows as if a bullet might hit him at any second. Considering Thirty-Six most likely knew, Gary was sure he had let Danny's drug-dealing happen for a reason. It was apparent everything connected to Thirty-Six had a purpose, although considering this brought unwanted attention to Danny's place of worship, if that's what it was, he'd love to know what that reason could be.

"Just take it easy," Gary said. "We'll be at my place in a few minutes. You look like you could use a shower ... and maybe a beer. And a shot."

"I could definitely use a drink," Danny said.

"What's your poison?"

"Beer is fine," Danny replied after a long pause, during which he constantly checked their surroundings.

"Any particular type?"

Another pause, "Nah. I'm easy," he said. After a while, he turned around, settled into his seat, and said, "You ever get that feeling like you're being watched? Or like how your hairs stand at attention when someone invades your personal space?"

Gary glanced over at Danny. "Sure. I guess," he said. Now that Danny had brought it up, Gary realized how perfect a description it was for the way he'd felt since Thirty-Six turned up in his bedroom that night a few months ago. As such, he hoped Danny wasn't going to mention Thirty-Six as it would validate that his own hair-raising case of eyes-on-him-itis was more than just a feeling.

"I can't shake it, man," Danny complained. "I can't see them, but it's like somehow I know they're out there, watching me."

It was obvious Danny was overloaded with anxiety, so Gary tried to offer some reassurance despite how unsettled he felt.

"I know how you feel," he said. "Trust me. Thirty-Six has a way of getting in your head. But you gotta relax or you'll drive yourself nuts."

Danny leaned back and closed his eyes as they hit the midtown tunnel. He took a couple of deep breaths, but Gary knew it would do little to relax him.

When they exited the tunnel, a truck backfired, causing Danny to jump up and bang his head on the roof of Gary's Honda Civic.

"It was just the SUV over there," Gary said, pointing to a beat-up looking Land Rover.

Danny rubbed his head and leaned back.

Five minutes later they parked and walked to Gary's apartment, Danny continually looking over his shoulder. Perhaps he should've just left him in jail? Maybe. But Gary intended to get as much info out of this guy as he could. After a few drinks he'd be open to talking.

It only took a few sips from a can of Pabst Blue Ribbon before Danny spilled everything. Gary had plopped down onto the couch, opened his beer, and barely had one sip before he started.

"I met Thirty-Six at an all-night film marathon, at a drive-in out on Long Island, just over a year ago. He was sitting in a lounge chair in the space next to me and my buddy in front of our cars, and his portable radio had better reception than ours. He put the radio down in front of us and told us to turn our 'piece of junk' off. We thanked him. He wouldn't accept a drink from us, or any of our snacks. But by the time the second feature had ended, he asked us what our favorite films were. He claimed he had never seen any of the Friday the 13th sequels. We had just watched Part Two and were getting ready for Part three to come on, but I found it hard to believe. After we told him our favorites, he began rattling off film titles I'd never heard of. They all sounded crazy, and a bit more extreme than I usually go for. But he had my interest. My buddy Chris tuned him out as soon as the movie started, but I kept talking with him throughout the film. I guess you can figure out the rest?"

"I think so," Gary said, sipping his beer. "Where did you see your first one?"

"The Bronx. Some warehouse. It took me a bit to get the money up, and when I arrived, I was $150.00 dollars short. I mean, four grand is a hell of a lot of money to come up with in a week."

"Wait," Gary said, "he gave you a week?"

"Yes."

"Weird. He told me he'd call me at any time within the next few days...then ended up calling me the same night we met."

"Holy shit."

"I had the cash and he knew it."

"Ah," Danny said, finished with his beer. "Mind if I have another?"

"Help yourself."

Danny drank half the can with two huge sips. "Anyway, I was hooked after the first film, but Thirty-Six knew I couldn't afford to see any more, at least not for a while. That's when he offered me a job."

Gary nodded. He wondered how Thirty-Six seemed to know so much about everyone and everything. It was apparent he knew about Danny before meeting him at that drive in, and he knew that Danny would work for him one day. That being the case, it stood to reason that his own meeting with Thirty-Six was completely designed by Thirty-Six himself.

Danny got up and grabbed a third beer and he sat down on the couch. He closed his eyes and said, "I wonder how long I have?"

Gary said nothing. They both knew he was living on borrowed time.

After opening a second beer, Gary finally asked, "Did Thirty-Six not pay you enough?"

"Huh?"

"The money? You mean to tell me Thirty-Six wasn't paying you enough? Why were you dealing dope?"

Danny rolled up his sleeve.

Needle marks ran up and down his left arm. "I started using to get what I saw out of my head."

Gary wanted to say, *You don't look strung out* or something along those lines, but decided not to.

"One thing led to another, and my supplier started offering me small jobs, which came in handy when Thirty-Six stopped calling me as much."

Gary realized he hadn't been called for a job in a while, but tried to shrug it off.

"He warned me to stay away from kids, and I did, but a couple of guys in a high-school punk band found out I sold, and they always had the cash when they came around. I shoulda known better. Fucking Gatekeepers have had a hard-on for bringing down the Satanic Church. Fuckers must've been following me."

"How'd you get involved with them?" Gary said. "The church, I mean?"

Danny let out a melancholic chuckle. "One of the guys who worked for Thirty-Six invited me to a meeting one night, and I figured why not? I was never a religious guy or anything, but I remembered reading about naked chicks, and drugs, and shit. Only, this place was nothing like that."

"After a couple of meetings, Thirty-Six began to give me more work," Danny continued. "I was starting to feel like I belonged to something. Like I mattered. As corny as it sounds, I hadn't felt that way in a long time. It was kinda nice. Ya know?"

"So, Thirty-Six is a member?"

"A member?" Danny laughed. "You mean you don't know?"

"Don't know what?"

Danny put his face in his hands, and then stood up and looked out the window. He was quiet for a few moments, which seemed like an eternity.

"Fuck it. I'm a dead man, anyway." Danny walked over to Gary, sat on the edge of the coffee table and looked him right in the eyes. "I guess I had earned their trust because, one night after a meeting at the church, I was shown a sacred text when I was let into their circle, the Circle of the Spinatae."

"Spinatae?"

"According to the text I was trusted to see, Thirty-Six is the Thirty-sixth guardian of hell itself... sort of like an avenging angel."

Gary's eyes widened.

"The Satanic Church is his front, most of the members his minions. They're on a mission to—"

"Wait! Hold that thought," Gary said, walking over to the book-shelf adjacent to his television, eager to follow-up on the thought that Danny's explanation, and more specifically, his mention of avenging angels. "Let me show you something."

Gary pulled a book from the shelf and took a moment to find a certain chapter. "Is this what you're about to tell me?"

Danny took the book and scanned the first two pages of the chapter. "Holy shit, how did you know?"

"I've been reading about this stuff since I was a kid. It was the inspiration for a script I wrote years ago. I never thought any of it was real, though."

"Well, it is, my friend," Danny said, handing the book back. "And now you're living it."

As he put the book back, Gary's expression bore the weight of Danny's statement. Somewhere beneath all that, he was annoyed Danny didn't follow up on his mention of script-writing, which Gary usually used as bait to elicit questions about his filmmaking ambitions.

"So, you know about the Reclamation, then?" Danny asked.

Gary said he was unfamiliar with the term.

"Really?" Danny said, looking surprised. "It's what they've been preparing for this whole time. I'd have thought Thirty-Six would've told you everything by now. Surely, he plans to bring you into the circle. Why else would he have hired you when he did?"

"What the fuck is the Reclamation?"

"It's when they take it all back."

"Take *what* back from *who*?"

Danny paused, and then he slowly unfurled his index finger until it pointed straight up at the ceiling.

Gary waited to be let in on the joke, but Danny looked deadly serious. He looked up at the ceiling, his mind drawing wild conclusions about biblical End-Times clichés.

"From... God?" Gary said, half-expecting Danny to laugh at his response. But Danny remained stone-face, nodding.

"The virus. The quarantine. It's all part of it," Danny elaborated. "It's the final step in their campaign to brainwash the masses through the media. Now they've got everyone in one place, addicted to their TV's, and phones, and computers. It's gonna be huge, man. Huge! One fell swoop, and *bam*! Life as we know it will never be the same."

After a few moments of drunken contemplation, Gary said, "Okay. So, let me get this straight..."

His phone buzzed, interrupting him.

**Tmrw morning. 9am. 126 Fairway Avenue. Great Neck, Long Island. Drive up to gate. You will be buzzed in. Y or N?**

*DEAR GOD*, Gary thought. He was certain Thirty-Six knew he was housing Danny, who had gone against the Circle of Spinatae's rules by revealing their plan to an outsider. Was this an actual job offer or was this his execution for helping the drug dealer? There wasn't a place on Earth he could run to. Gary was never more aware of that fact. He texted back Y and tucked his phone into his back pocket.

"That was him, wasn't it," Danny asked.

"It was."

"He's looking for me, isn't he?"

Gary turned around and shrugged. "Probably. But this was an offer for tomorrow morning."

"Did you accept?"

"I did. I haven't worked on a shoot in weeks."

Danny laughed. "And the night you bail my ass out you get a gig."

Gary reached for another beer. He took a sip, saw Danny motion for one, and tossed him a can. "And if it's not a real gig, there isn't a goddamn thing I can do about it."

"Then we're both fucked."

Danny filled Gary in on the details of the Reclamation as they sat in the apartment's low lighting and sipped their beers. That Thirty-Six had neglected to tell him all this made Gary even more nervous about the shoot tomorrow.

They sipped in silence for a while. Danny was trembling as he chugged from his can, and it stole some of his composure. Not that he had much to offer at the moment.

An hour later both men passed out, Danny on the floor, Gary slouched in the La-Z-Boy upon which he had spent countless hours nestled in while watching his favorite films. But their nerves wouldn't allow them to rest for long.

## 13

It made Gary feel like a rebel that he was one of very few cars on the road...or an idiot. It was a fleeting thing that popped up between extended periods of deep contemplation that made the drive to Great Neck seem to take only seconds.

Great Neck, Long Island was a high-income neighborhood. As he drove by houses that must've started in the seven-digits, with driveways housing multiple vehicles, each worth more than most people made in a year, Gary wondered why they had decided to shoot there. He also wondered if Danny was still alive. Apparently, he had left sometime during the night, nowhere to be found when Gary woke up this morning. That, or he was taken.

Gary thought of the Reclamation, and about how he could possibly fit into it, before blowing it off as drunk conspiracy-talk. Surely there were much more pragmatic motives at the root of Thirty-Six.

Gary was more concerned with the very real possibility that he might be walking into a set-up that could result in his own extremely painful demise.

He thought of the money he had saved to date, roughly 15 grand.

Not enough for a feature, but he could use half of it to make a hell of a short film, then the other half to promote the shit out of it.

In the end, Gary refused to fully accept that Thirty-Six would do anything to harm him as he felt there was a genuine kinship between them as connoisseurs of horror cinema. And, quiet as it's kept, Gary was becoming desensitized to the violence.

Maybe that was Thirty-Six's plan all along.

Gary made a right onto Fairway Avenue and looked for the address texted to him. 126 was five houses in. He slowed, pulled into the driveway, then went several feet further to a tall iron gate. He lowered his window and heard a faint electric hum. He followed the sound and saw a small camera turning his way. A red light on the top of it flashed, confirming his identity. Then the gate opened, eerily silent. Gary felt as if he was in a James Bond film, and half-expected to be greeted at the front door by a bald, British man, with a nasty facial scar, petting a cat.

Instead, Gary saw Handsome Hugo waiting as soon as he pulled into the only open parking spot, alongside six other cars. The front yard was huge and very well kept no doubt by the most expensive landscapers in the area.

Gary nodded. Thirty-Six's favorite bouncer, as Gary thought of him, nodded back, and he followed another man he had never seen before through a meticulously furnished mansion. The new man was dressed like a butler for some 80s, postmodern Bohemian, philan-thropist-type, and seemed pleased that Gary didn't ask him anything. There was a bulge in the man's shirt at the small of his back.

Gary took in the artwork that lined the walls, the sculptures nearly every five feet, and even some gold records which hung in strategic places. He couldn't see what bands were on the record labels, and wondered if Thirty-Six had something going with a famous musician, possibly even an artist or band that he knew of. Gary was starting to feel like Mark Wahlberg's character in the film *Rock Star*, one his few non-horror favorites.

The new man stopped at a door somewhere in what Gary assumed was the center of the house.

"Please watch your head," he said as he stepped into a narrow stairway.

Gary counted the steps as they descended to the poorly lit basement. By the time they reached the bottom, he had counted twenty-seven, which felt like a bit much for a residential home. But then again, nothing remotely connected to Thirty-Six seemed normal.

The new man led him to a well-lit room, where the same camera and lights he had used on the previous films were set up. Aside from an old kitchen table in the center, and a large gang box on the left-hand side, the area was bare.

"Glad you could make this one," Thirty-Six said, appearing on Gary's left side. "We're all becoming big fans of your work, Gary... excuse me. *Lee.*"

At first Gary was startled, wondering where the hell he had come from and why he hadn't even heard his shoes slapping against the cement floor. And then he thought of what Danny had told him.

"We're just about ready," one of the armed assistants yelled from a doorway at the far end of the shooting area.

"Very good," Thirty-Six said, putting his hand on Gary's shoulder. "Today you're in for something special, and by something special... never mind. You'll see in a couple of minutes."

Gary's shoulder felt incredibly cold the second Thirty-Six removed his hand from it.

"We'll be shooting by and around that table," he said, pointing to the center of the room. "Take a few minutes to adjust to whatever angles you'll be most comfortable with. Then let us know when you're ready."

"Okay," Gary said, wondering why he was being given so much freedom compared to the previous shoots. He was particularly focused on the part where he was to tell *them* when *he* was ready. And as he fiddled with the lens, zooming in and out of the center of the table, he felt as if he had been given a promotion within this demented organization.

Gary was ready in less than two minutes. He cracked his knuckles, wiped his sweaty palms on his pants. "I'm all set," he said.

Thirty-Six walked out from a side room. "Very good." He handed Gary an outfit that looked like the one Michael Myers wore in the *Halloween* films, only it was black instead of blue, and a black leather mask with eye holes and two smaller holes for the nose. Nothing for the mouth. "Put these on."

Another man stepped up to the camera, peeked through the viewfinder and said, "Fantastic. This should be perfect," giving Gary a thumbs up.

An assistant entered the room and began to dress in the same outfit Gary was given.

"Is there a problem?" Thirty-Six asked when he noticed Gary hadn't even started to put the outfit on yet.

"Not at all," Gary said as he began to undress, then step into the bondage-meets-goth get up.

"Today," Thirty-Six said, "you're going to prove your loyalty to us, Gary." And then, acting as the director, Thirty-Six said to two other assistants standing nearby, "You two stay out of shot. A prop will be brought in, and someone will be placed inside the prop." He turned to Gary and the assistant. "You two will use this to cut the prop in half."

He opened the gang box and removed an old fashioned two-man saw. It was rusty and reminded Gary of a Shark's jaw.

That he had now been cast as "talent" in this film made Gary sweat under the mask. He knew what was about to happen, and he had a choice to make: go through with it and live, or attempt to flee and die. He knew he'd never make it out of the basement, and even if he did, where would he go? To the police? Knowing Thirty-Six, he probably had a few of them in his pocket, as well.

Gary and the assistant nodded, the cameraman nodded, and Thirty-Six waited for what seemed like an hour before shouting, "Action!"

Gary heard the camera roll. There were a few moments of inactivity, as if done deliberately to build suspense.

Gary was wound so tightly that he nearly jumped out of his shoes when two men entered the room, dressed in the same outfits that he and the assistant wore. They worked together to carry a hollowed-out log from its ends. It must've been 10-feet-long.

*Dear God,* Gary thought, knowing full-well what was about to happen.

And sure enough, after the log was set atop the table and secured with thick rope, the men left the room, coming back with a body that had been stuffed inside a burlap sack.

They emptied the sack onto the floor.

It was Danny. He was completely naked, his wrists and ankles duct taped. Another strip of duct-tape covered his mouth.

The look of terror on Danny's face made Gary want to puke.

Somehow, Gary kept his composure as the men slid the writhing, bucking victim feet-first into the log. The duct-tape did a fine job muffling Danny's horror.

One of the men eventually shoved Danny's head in as if stuffing a Thanksgiving turkey, and the log barely budged despite the spastic, futile wriggling coming from within.

When the two men left, the assistant walked toward the table. Gary was in tow, his heart racing as if he had just snorted a dozen eight-balls of pure Columbian and sprinted around the Earth twice. He felt as if he might pass out as he took one side of the log.

The assistant rested the saw atop the log and waited for Gary to take hold of the handle on his end.

Gary breathed as deeply as he could, trying desperately not to lose his shit. He wasn't a murderer, but he'd be murdered if he didn't do this. He figured he'd let the assistant do most of the cutting and he'd try his best to play along, but as they cut into the log, Gary knew he'd have to pull his weight or they'd never get to the body inside.

As they broke through the first layer of log, he accepted that this was his punishment for helping Danny. They continued sawing. Gary was sweating profusely. The back of his costume was saturated and clinging to his skin. He could feel the sweat running down his ass and soaking his boxers.

Danny's muffled screams intensified as the blade made contact with his chest. At least Gary assumed they were cutting across his chest. Or maybe it was his waist. Within a minute, blood began to trickle from the point in the log where the saw worked back and forth like a piston from hell. Another minute and blood was pouring from both ends of the log.

Gary closed his eyes and pretended he was at home with his ex-girlfriend Karen, making love, or even watching some corny Hallmark Channel film starring one of five vaguely familiar starlets and a revolving door of non-threatening, overly manicured pretty-boys. At that moment, when Danny had stopped squirming and screaming into his gag, Gary thought that he'd give anything to actually be back with Karen, watching whatever shitty chick-flick or vapid reality show she wanted to watch. As these thoughts started to take him out of his current situation, he felt as if he wasn't alone in his own head.

Gary opened his eyes and squinted to see past the blinding camera lights. He caught a glimpse of Thirty-Six staring back at him and nodding, a knowing look on his face.

There was an uncanny intensity behind Thirty-Six's eyes that Gary found strangely intoxicating even in the presence of acute, white-knuckle fear. He looked away, which was more difficult than it should have been. With his body on autopilot, continuing to saw, he considered the odd shape of Thirty-Six's shadow cast long and slender on the wall behind him, more human-like than human. When he glanced again, careful to avoid the force-of-nature-of-a-man who cast the shadow in question, it looked normal.

Gary was startled when the log they had been sawing finally split in two. Half fell on the floor. The other half remained on the table. Gary looked down as best he could through the small eye holes and realized he and his sawing partner were covered in Danny's blood.

Gary took a step back as the assistant motioned for him to take hold of the saw. Then the assistant lifted the remaining log off the table.

Danny's head rolled out, hitting the cement floor with a sickening *splat*. The expression frozen on his face conveyed a level of terror that reached deep down into Gary's chest and siphoned all the warmth from his body.

They hadn't been cutting through Danny's chest or abdomen after all. They had sawed clean through his neck.

When they were finished shooting, Gary walked into a back room and pulled his mask off. He felt extremely nauseous, but he wasn't about to give Thirty-Six or his crew the satisfaction of seeing him puke. He held it in, breathed deeply, and grabbed one of several folded chairs leaning against the wall, opened it, and sat down. The damp basement air felt like a cool fall afternoon compared to having that damn mask on.

Thirty-Six entered the back room. He grabbed a chair from the leaning stack and sat facing Gary. "I appreciate not having to explain things to you," He said, and patted Gary's shoulder. "From here on out, keep out of my business. Understood?"

"Understood."

"Good," Thirty-Six said as he stood back up. "Because I like you much better behind the camera. Your acting stinks."

Gary watched Thirty-Six leave the room laughing, his heart still racing.

Later, the assistant collected Gary's bloodied outfit in a thick, black bag, then led him to a shower room.

Gary stood under the hot water shaking, unable to erase the terrified look on Danny's face when his head fell out of the log and hit the cement floor, and then Thirty-Six's eyes bearing down on him as he sawed away, and his peculiar shadow, from of his mind.

It was going to be a very long night.

# 14

Gary spent the next week in his apartment. He hadn't called in to work and didn't care about the repercussions. He slept like shit, barely ate, and kept CNN on just for background noise. Ninety nine percent of the news was devoted to the pandemic. 809,608 infected globally as of March 31st. The United States had the most confirmed cases of the virus, with 189,000, and 3,900 deaths. The experts were forecasting New York as the next likely hotspot. Currently the death toll was at 1,096 and climbing exponentially every day.

The talking heads conveyed uplifting testaments to human decency as a means of distracting millions of quarantined viewers from the ominous prognoses of the doctors and nurses on the front line, and the egg-head scientists. Bottom line: things were going to get much worse before they got better.

Every last morsel of information was repeated ad nauseam during the 24-hour news cycle. Eventually, the background noise graduated to prominence in the shitstorm of stress-inducing thoughts that swirled around Gary's head. He remembered what Danny had said about the virus being part of the church's plan, and suddenly, it didn't seem out of the realm of possibility.

He shuddered at the ghastly images that followed: Danny's severed head rolling out of the log, the expression on his face, and the sickening *splat* sound it made when it hit the cement floor.

*Time to change the channel.*

Gary opted for the Hallmark Channel instead as it instantly reminded him of Karen, which gave him some degree of comfort. He spent hours, days it seemed, lost in his thoughts staring blankly at the screen as hastily made flicks about overzealous exes, murderous babysitters, and wrongly convicted mommies on the lam played out in front of him.

At some point, Gary managed to get off his ass. He pulled one of his old occult volumes from the bookshelf and began to look for info on the Spinatae.

It took four different books and nearly two hours of reading, but Danny had been right. Members of the Spinatae were indeed reputed to be "avenging angels," sort of hell's "Repo Division," assigned to locate and collect lost souls who had somehow managed to escape their eternal prison and return to Earth, able to live inside innocent hosts.

And each one of them was numbered.

Some accounts said thousands existed across the world, which made Gary wonder how many lost souls could've escaped hell. He read on, pulling everything he had on demonology and Satanism off his shelves, searching as if he'd somehow find the key to defeating Thirty-Six, or at least getting him off his back.

Gary took a quick break and grabbed a can of beer. As he sipped, he wondered why Thirty-Six had seemed to take a liking to him in the first place, and if he was ever going to make good on his promise to help him re-start his "legitimate" film career. If Thirty-Six really was a demon incarnate, perhaps he was simply lying to Gary, happy to be using someone who genuinely loved film as part of his evil crew. But that was a big "if."

And why were they filming all this? Why not just kill these bastards and send them back to hell? Why were they creating entertainment out of what these books claimed they had been ordered to do by a higher power?

Gary finished his beer and grabbed another. He sat back down and prepared to read further. After yawning his way through the next couple of pages, he decided that he'd rather read in bed. A quick bite to eat and a shower, and he'd be good for another chapter or so.

Gary made himself a sandwich which he inhaled, afterwards hitting the shower. As he stood beneath the scalding water, he laughed nervously at the thought that he was pretty much now working for hell itself. He was still chuckling as he wrapped a towel around his waist and headed to the bedroom.

He flicked the light on and walked over to his dresser. He grabbed a pair of sweats from the bottom drawer, unwrapped the towel from around his waist, and let it fall to the floor.

"Looking good," came a voice from behind.

Gary spun around, wondering who the hell had snuck into his apartment *this time.*

Gary's ex, Karen, whom he hadn't seen in over a year, stood up from the bed with nothing on, a hip-length designer trench coat in a heap at her feet. She looked hotter than he remembered, and it was obvious that she had been working out. Not that she was ever out of shape, but as she approached him she looked slimmer, more toned.

And there was a twinkle in her eye that seemed...*otherworldly.*

Gary was simultaneously embarrassed and aroused. He immediately covered himself with his arms and backed away from her until the dresser obstructed his movement.

"H...How did you get in here?" he asked.

"If it's a bad time, I can leave," Karen said in a playful deadpan.

"No, It's just that I didn't expect—"

"I've seen you a couple of times in the street. Seems like things are going well for you."

"Huh?"

*She's talking about your new threads, dumbass.*

"Finally caught a break, I guess you can say," he said, not wanting to reveal too much.

"Well. Success suits you."

Before he could thank her, Karen slid to her knees, moved his arms from in front of his erect penis, and looking him directly in the eyes, began to lick the tip. "Have you missed me as much as I've missed you?" she said.

As Gary grew more erect, he couldn't help but remember how *she* had split on *him,* yet her entire demeanor seemed to say she thought it was the other way around. Gary was quite sure she was here either under instruction of Thirty-Six, or, as she took his entire penis into her mouth without the slightest gag, by the *possession* of him or one of the Spinatae? The thought made him shiver and slightly softened his erection. He thought of Danny, then the poor bastard in the dog cage, and every other atrocity that he had been forced to film and now perform in, and his erection softened more.

Karen sucked more vigorously, rolling her tongue along the shaft, making loud, slurping sounds, and whipping her head back and forth, and before Gary knew it, the bad thoughts were washed away by a surge of pure ecstasy that made his knees buckle and his legs turn to jelly. It was almost as if she had done it purposely to get his mind off of Thirty-Six.

Karen released him at the precipice of a monumental orgasm, stood up, and started licking his neck. "I've really, really missed you," she said, yanking him closer with both hands.

"I've missed you too," he answered in a breathy murmur, his voice trembling with lust.

She walked Gary over to the bed, laid down on her back, and spread her legs. Gary climbed on top of her. She was soaking wet, and he easily slid inside. He pumped away for a full hour it seemed, but to his amazement, he didn't come, and felt as if he wouldn't for a while.

"AND THE OSCAR GOES TO...LEE Revok!"

The announcement was followed by applause and cheers, and schmaltzy, awards-show, celebratory music.

Gary opened his eyes.

He was in a grand auditorium decorated to elicit nostalgia for the Golden Age of Hollywood. He moved, as if on wheels, down a long narrow aisle, toward a pair of presenters awaiting his arrival atop a wide spit-shined stage. A large screen hanging high on the rear stage-wall ran clips from the winning film—a cinema verité-style montage of grindhouse meets technophobia, meets satanic-panic doomsday images that ended with the title AT MIDNIGHT WE POSSESS THE DAMNED in bold white lettering against a black screen.

On either side of him, a standing ovation from people he recognized from movies and TV.

Gary reached the stage, and transcended the steps as if he were rolling up a ramp. He moved toward a woman who was the spitting-image of Catriona MacColl as she looked in Fulci's heyday. Or maybe it *was* her. It was a face that had fueled many a masturbatory session. As such, it made Gary's dick hard. She cradled the Oscar in her arms, smiling as if she held Gary in high regard. They embraced and she handed him the statue. Gary approached the clear podium, over-flowing with a sense of accomplishment that was beyond anything he ever imagined in his most optimistic Hollywood fantasy.

The ovation went on and on. As Gary stood there, marinating in the adulation, he scanned the crowd for more noteworthy faces. He glimpsed some of his favorites: Fulci, Bava, Argento, Romero, Gordon Lewis, Cronenberg, Carpenter.

Down in front was the pedophiliac priest from the first real snuff film he had seen. He was nothing but a torso and a pile of limbs placed in a seat next to the "talent" from *Eaten Alive, Burning Man, Pin Cushion,* and *Skin Deep.* They clapped and cheered despite being dismembered, gnawed-and-chewed, burnt-to-a-crisp, pierced-to-shit, and peeled like an orange.

After several minutes, the applause subsided and the audience took their seats. The room fell silent as a hundred plus faces waited for Gary to speak.

His stomach in knots, Gary took a deep breath, cleared his throat, and...

Somewhere, in the heart of the crowd, a man shot to his feet and stole the room's attention. It was Danny. He was headless, a jagged stump atop his shoulders, white t-shirt stained dark red around the neck and upper torso. Danny held his head out in front of him, clutching it by the hair. A look of grave concern on his face. Moving in slow motion, he pointed toward the exit at the back of the auditorium and yelled, but there were no words. Heads turned to face him. Gary leaned forward and squinted, attempting to read Danny's lips.

"Run! You must get away! They're coming for you!"

Gary's eyes fluttered open and he lay there, face-down in the pillow, while his brain rebooted. He laughed at the absurdity of dreams and then smiled at the comforting thought of Karen lying next to him.

"You awake?" he mumbled.

"Mm. Hmm," she cooed, a few seconds later.

"Listen. This is gonna sound crazy, but what if we got the hell outta Dodge? Just the two of us. I've got enough money saved. We could get a place, and just kinda start over...the way it should've been before we broke up."

He paused for a response, but then the floodgates swung open and several weeks' worth of bottled-up anxiety came pouring out.

"I got myself in *way* over my head with some pretty heavy shit. The things I've seen...that I've done...If I told you, you'd think I was nuts. Maybe I am. I don't know. I guess I convinced myself that I could live with it as long as I wasn't directly involved. But this last time..." he began to well up, thinking of Danny. "If you coulda seen the look on his face...he was just a kid."

Gary caught himself spiraling and took a deep breath.

"I'm sorry. It's just that, when I saw you again, it made me realize that I can't do this anymore. I wish I could tell you more, but I don't want you to think bad of me."

Thinking he had already said too much, Gary reached blindly for the warmth of Karen's naked body but found an empty space instead. He panicked, and turned his head reluctantly, confirming that he was, in fact, alone in bed. But he had clearly heard her respond when he asked if she was awake. Or so he thought.

*No way was Karen a dream, too. No fucking way!*

It was dark and there was a stillness in the air. As Gary listened, he could hear the TV blaring from the living room. It sounded like chaos. Angry crowds. Protests. Rioting. A concerned female reporter struggled to speak through a mask and over the cacophony of noise.

"We've often speculated, and usually with tongue firmly planted in cheek, about the effects of a sudden global Internet crash," said the reporter, "but I don't think anyone could have imagined what we've been seeing from around the world in the few hours since that very thing has happened."

But the reporter might as well have been speaking Mandarin, as Gary was solely focused on his memory of turning the TV off before he started reading last night.

*Karen*, he assumed, excitedly. She was probably in there, lounging on the couch after raiding his fridge for a snack or a glass of water. He checked the clock on his nightstand, squinting at the bright red letters slicing through the darkness. 3:44 am. Feeling quite good about himself, Gary rolled onto his back and waited for his eyes to adjust.

As the layout of his bedroom solidified, so did four looming shapes, like dark columns arched over him on all sides. It took his brain a moment to register that they were people. Four of them, dressed in all black, with clear masks over their faces. Gary knew the outfit well, and it scared the shit out of him.

"Oh my god!" Gary yelled as the four assistants grabbed him by the wrists and ankles and tried to hold him still. "Hey, Wait! What the fuck is going on?"

But Gary knew exactly what was going on. It was worst-case-scenario, numero uno.

"No! Wait! Please!" he yelled, kicking and wriggling. "I didn't do anything!" And when they didn't answer and continued to restrain him, he said, "Please! Just tell me what I did?"

"You know what you did," said one of the assistants, Gary couldn't tell which. And then, one of the men jabbed him in the ribs with a Taser.

Gary cried out, bucking and flexing in response to the electric sucker-punch to every single cell in his body. The assistant held the Taser against Gary's ribs, but he resisted. He was trying to tell them that he didn't know what he did, but all that came out was groaning gibberish.

Through the mind-scrambling surge of wattage that warped his vision fuzzy, Gary saw one of assistants reach behind his back and pull a pistol from his waist.

"No!" Gary grunted, his struggle intensifying.

The assistant let go of Gary and the others took up the slack. Looking down at him, his head cocked to the side as if he was amused by Gary's struggle-dance, the assistant flipped the gun in his hand and hit Gary over the head with the butt.


GARY CAME to in a drunken haze, his head throbbing fiercely as his brain labored to course correct. As the disorienting effects of blunt-force slumber began to melt away, he realized that he was in the backseat of a car. Something big and spacious, that an old churchy black man might drive. Maybe a Buick or a Lincoln Town Car. He was naked. His thighs and buttocks stuck to the seat, and it was so quiet that he could hear his skin peeling from the vinyl whenever his weight shifted. He was sandwiched between two assistants dressed in black. Two others sat in the driver's and passenger seats. All wearing masks. They stunk of cigarettes and the kind of cologne your average douchebag might wear to a club.

It was 4:15 am according to the scrolling text above the storefront window they passed. The streets were alive with activity. The ghostly echo of distant police sirens bounced between buildings as people wandered about holding smartphones, tablets, and laptops up over their heads in desperate search of a signal, with little-to-no concern for masks or social distancing.

Crowds formed outside closed coffee-shops, cafés, bookstores, and any other business that doubled as a WIFI hotspot. People sat on front stoops looking lost, some flat-out weeping. Infected people among the throng of hysterical folks took breaks to puke and defecate in alleyways, or in plain sight when the matter arose unexpected.

People stood on sidewalks yelling warnings and conspiracy theories at passing vehicles. The driver had to swerve to avoid hitting a disheveled man carrying a sign that read *Welcome to the Apocalypse, Bitches!*

For a moment, Gary thought he might be dreaming again. And then he remembered Karen, and his stomach sank.

"Karen," he said sheepishly. "Is she alright?"

"Who?" said the assistant to his right, who was quickly admonished by the driver.

"The woman who was there with me?" Gary added. There was no response.

Gary hoped that Karen had left sometime before they arrived, which under different circumstances, would have left him feeling dejected. He wondered if they had harmed her in some way, or worse —that she was in on it, that she was just a figment of his imagination, somehow orchestrated by Thirty-Six.

They drove in absolute silence, seemingly unaffected by the chaos outside. They passed a small huddle of people entranced by a flatscreen TV hanging in the window of an otherwise dark electronics store.

On the screen, a reporter stood outside the headquarters of the country's largest Internet Service Provider, looking as if he feared for his safety from the unruly, mostly maskless crowd of ordinary people that had gathered by the front doors searching for answers. Beneath him, a BREAKING NEWS banner with the sub-head, *MASS HYSTERIA ERUPTS OVER WORLDWIDE INTERNET CRASH!*

The assistant in the passenger seat turned to the driver and said, "It's happening just like he said it would."

The driver nodded.

"Listen, guys," Gary said, trying to reach at least one of them, thinking that there had to be another Danny in the bunch. "I don't know what I did wrong, but I promise you, whatever it was, it was a mistake."

No response.

"Is it because of Danny?"

Nothing.

"Because me and Thirty-Six are square on that," he tried to assure them. "We talked about it at the last shoot."

"I can give you money," he said, addressing all of them, in desperation. "More than *he's* paying you, I bet. Danny told me that he doesn't pay you much."

As long as they didn't ask for more than $28,876 combined, which was the sum of Gary's earnings from the films thus far, plus his savings. Hell, even if they did ask for more, with the way he felt right now, he'd find a way to make it happen.

Gary exhaled in defeat when no one as much as flinched at his offer. He sat back and stared straight ahead, ignoring the surreal scene beyond the windshield, mind suddenly blank. Then, out of nowhere, a ghastly montage of possibilities pertaining to his own painful death at the hands of Thirty-Six scrolled through his mind, and suddenly, he longed for his clothing or, at the very least, a blanket to make him feel less exposed and vulnerable. He began to hyperventilate and feel nauseous.

It gave Gary an idea. If he threw up all over these guys, they'd probably stop the car and jump out. Anybody would. That might give him a chance to run. There were people everywhere. There's no way the assistants would chase him with so many eyes on them.

Gary closed his eyes and let the nausea gestate. It didn't take long before he began to lurch. He felt something against his knee and looked down to see that the assistant on his right was pressing the barrel of his Glock against it.

"You do it, and I'll pull you outta this fucking car and shoot you in the kneecaps," he said in a raspy, hateful voice.

The assistant with the gun looked up at his masked colleagues, who were all looking at him.

"Thirty-Six said he wants him *alive*," the man said as if he felt their silent criticism. "A bullet to the kneecaps wouldn't *kill* him."

Gary's involuntary visualization of the man's threat was just the inspiration he needed to purge the contents of his stomach. He threw up all over the back of the driver seat and the center console.

In the woozy moments to follow, Gary heard profanities, and the sound of brakes squealing. All four doors flung open, and he felt suddenly unencumbered on both sides. But Gary was in shock, and in no condition to run.

One of the assistants leaned back into the car, mumbling a string of expletives. He cocked his arm back and...

## 15

G ary awoke tied to a chair, his head slumped painfully forward. He was still naked, but his embarrassment was a non-factor. There were voices all around him. Movement. The skin around his right eye was tight and throbbing. The restraints around his wrists and ankles cut off his circulation. He wanted badly to lift his head and massage away the soreness at the back of his neck. Instead, he kept his eyes closed, head slumped forward, and listened.

He quickly deciphered from the noise all around him, and from the sound of Thirty-Six's voice supervising the process, that they were setting up for a shoot.

He had to concentrate to keep from trembling. He ventured further, fantasizing that if he concentrated hard enough, he could wish himself away from here. Thinking in happy place cliches, Gary envisioned himself lounging on a tropical beach with Karen, sipping pina coladas, or some such frou-frou drink from a coconut. And just as quickly as the image materialized in his mind, it was snatched away by a brief exchange of words overheard in the present.

"We're ready to start, sir," said a male voice, presumably belonging to an assistant. "Should we wake him up?"

"No need. He's already awake," Thirty-Six replied. "Isn't that right, Gary?"

Gary felt that Thirty-Six calling him by his real name only made things worse. He maintained the unconscious act, mostly to stall for time as if a few seconds longer would allow for some miracle to materialize from thin air.

*It's okay to be afraid, Gary,* said a voice in his head, Thirty-Six's voice. *In fact, I'd prefer that you are. It'll make for a more lively performance.*

Gary's eyes shot open and a string of desperate pleas poured from his mouth.

"Please don't do this," he said. "Whatever it is you think I did, I assure you it must be some kind of mistake."

"I wish that were true, Gary. I was really hoping that we could be friends."

"But... we *are* friends!"

"I *thought* we were. I thought you understood what we're doing here, that you wanted to be a part of it."

"But I *do* understand! I *do* want to be a part of it!"

"Is that right?" Thirty-Six said as if he held a trump-card in his back pocket, motioning to someone standing in Gary's peripheral.

He subconsciously assessed the room in the seconds before an assistant side-stepped into view clutching a rolled stack of papers.

He was in the remains of what looked like an old theater comprised of High Victorian Gothic-style architecture underneath a layer of damp mold and soot-colored film. There were assistants hauling refuse into piles at the feet of a pair of gothic pillars on either side of the room, setting up lighting, sound, and multiple cameras. The whole thing was unlike Thirty-Six, who usually worked with one camera set-up and a skeleton crew of five or six, tops.

The place was littered with the corpses of uprooted wooden chairs, skeletal remains of hospital furniture, and miscellaneous trash from a bygone era. A large space had been cleared in the middle of the room, which is where Gary sat facing an old stage, upon which a twelve-foot wooden cross lay propped at an angle. A thick braid of wires wrapped around the cross's center support, from top-to-bottom, and snaked across the stage to a portable generator on wheels sitting off to the side.

Gary quickly clocked all the potential escape routes. Two sets of double doors on the left and a large doorless opening on the right, a ramped walkway extending down into a dark corridor. He suspected there was an exit in the back of the room as well, but couldn't turn his head to confirm it.

The ghosts of stenciled letters on a side wall read, *KIRKBRIDE AUDITORIUM*. An old, sun-cooked, black and white photograph of the Hudson River State Hospital in a cracked frame, was propped amongst the rubbish-pile.

*The old place in Poughkeepsie?* Following its closure in the early 2000s, the building had become a hotspot for the homeless, vandals, and weekend-arsonists.

The assistant next to Thirty-Six unfurled the paper stack with a snap and started reading.

"Page three, paragraph five: recipient will not disclose confidential information to any person or entity without the prior consent of the owner. Failure to adhere to this agreement is punishable by death."

Gary's face creased with fear.

"But I didn't tell anyone,"he said. "I swear!"

Thirty-Six interrupted, repeating what he had told Karen last night, verbatim.

Gary didn't think his heart could sink any lower. Clobbered by regret, his posture deflated.

*I should've known*, he thought, remembering the fine print that he didn't bother to read before signing the contract.

"But she won't tell anyone!" he said.

"That's not the point, Gary."

Gary thought for a moment.

"You can't just lay all this shit on someone and expect them not to have a moment of weakness!" he said.

"I can, and I do. I thought you understood that."

"But I..." *Do understand,* he started to say, but was stopped by a mental image of Karen in distress.

"Karen. Is she alright?" Gary asked.

Thirty-Six hesitated, cracked a sly smile.

"I'd assume that the *real* Karen is living her life just fine without you," he said.

*The real Karen?* Gary's brow furrowed as his mind rounded the corner to a sobering realization that he feared might be true.

"You *were* behind that, weren't you?" he muttered feebly, as if it hurt him physically to say it.

Thirty-Six straightened his posture and placed a hand over his chest. He raised the other hand like a witness preparing to be sworn in to testify in court, and like it was all a big joke, said, "I plead the fifth."

Gary, devastated, slumped in the chair as much as the restraints would allow. "But why?" he whimpered.

"Call it a test," Thirty-Six shot right back. "One that came wrapped in a gift, because I like you."

"But that's not fair."

"Fair?" Thirty-Six replied like the word was foreign to him, and then laughed heartily. "I'm the 36th guardian of hell. Do I play fair?"

Hearing Thirty-Six say it put any doubt to rest about hell, the Devil, and all the things that go bump in the night in his service, and it stole what little bit of hope that Gary had left.

He looked up to stave off the tears and was startled by a chipped and faded replica of Michelangelo's *The Creation of Adam* that spanned the entire ceiling. Looking on the painting with reverent awe, Gary began to pray.

*Please God, don't let me die. Not like this.*

And then he lowered his head and wept.

Thirty-Six looked rather proud of himself as he watched Gary come apart at the seams. He checked his watch and said, "As much as I'd like to stay here and chat with you, Gary, time is of the essence."

He placed a hand on Gary's shoulder, leaned in close. "For what it's worth," he whispered, "it's been fun."

Thirty-Six walked away, and a few seconds later, a pair of assistants began working to free Gary from the restraints.

He resisted as soon as he felt the restraints loosen, thinking it his only chance at escaping, but the assistants adjusted as if they had expected that very reaction.

The assistant on the left buried a fist in his gut, just below the sternum. Gary cried out and fell limp, coughing and gasping for air as the assistants dragged him by the armpits up to the stage.

Gary could only moan in protest. His lungs couldn't fill with enough air to support a more spirited and intelligible objection as the assistants guided him up the short staircase and onto the stage.

One of the assistants held his limp, ragdoll frame while the other one hurried offstage, returning with a ball-peen hammer and a fistful of eight-inch landscape spikes.

Gary knew what they were to be used for and moaned accordingly.

The assistant put the hammer and spikes on the floor and helped drag Gary up to the cross, turn him around, and place his back against the center support.

"No. Wait," Gary managed, making his arms rigid so the assistants had a difficult time controlling him. "Please don't do this! Please!"

The assistants slammed him against the wooden structure, which shook from the impact. The assistant on the right exploded into a fit of rage and punched Gary in the face several times, which he barely felt, due to his spiking adrenaline. He did, however, taste blood. The assistant balled his fist and cocked his arm back to administer another blow.

Gunshots, several of them in rapid succession, echoed from the mouth of the ramped corridor that opened into the auditorium.

The assistants let go of Gary, and he collapsed to the floor. They snatched their handguns from their waists and aimed at the doorless entrance. The other assistants did the same.

The stage-floor was cold, and it reminded Gary that he was naked. Lying on the floor, Gary spotted Thirty-Six standing behind Handsome Hugo, who had his arm out as if to protect him or to obstruct his forward movement. He glimpsed a hint of concern in Thirty-Six's expression, an emotion Gary previously thought him incapable of.

Seconds later, the ramped corridor coughed out two assistants who stumble-ran into the large room as if injured and fleeing for their lives. A barrage of gunfire from deeper in the corridor produced a lightshow of muzzle flashes that gave the assistants' bullet-dance a somewhat artful appearance.

There was a brief silence before soldiers emerged from the corridor in sleek, white paramilitary gear, armed with automatic weapons, eyes peeking out from behind snug, white hoods, the familiar Gatekeepers seal emblazoned on the upper right breast of their uniforms.

The assistants sunk into firing stances and took aim as the regimen of twenty-odd Gatekeepers fanned out into the room and stood side-by-side.

At the back of the formation, a dark-skinned man emerged. The contrast between his smooth, dark skin, and the gleaming white slim-fit suit that wrapped his sinewy frame was striking. He had long dreads fashioned into a messy bun.

It was the Jamaican from the Stor-right and Luxemburg YMCA shoots.

*What the hell is he doing with the Gatekeepers?* Gary thought.

A pair of soldiers stepped forward and stood on either side of the Jamaican. Their uniforms suggested a higher rank than the others. A thick nylon strap wrapped diagonally around the soldier on the right's torso, holding a long bulky gun against his back, the butt peeking over his shoulder. The soldier on the left held a tablet of some sort down by his side.

"I see that you haven't changed, brother," the Jamaican said self-assured, his accent heavy.

Thirty-Six's face cycled through emotions. His eyes narrowed and he walked out from behind Handsome Hugo, hands clasped behind his back, his expression stoic with a fire simmering underneath. He took a deep breath out of frustration, or annoyance, and then unclasped his hands and aimed a slow clap at the Jamaican.

"Hats off to you, brother," he said, feigning calm. "I can usually sniff out your spies. But you got one past me this time."

"Your arrogance blinds you to a great many things."

"All that 'my way or the highway' Kool-Aid that *Big Baddy Never-wrong* up there has got you boy scouts drinking..." his face twisted angry. "...and *I'm* the arrogant one? For what? Doing my job?"

"Attempting to circumvent that which is prophesied does not fall within your purview, brother," the Jamaican said.

"Attempting to circumvent that which is prophesied does not fall within your purview," Thirty-Six mocked in a silly voice.

Then, he shot a glare at Gary that made him shudder.

"He breached the contract. Plain and simple," said Thirty-Six. "What he might *mean* to Space Daddy isn't my concern."

Gary lingered on that part, wondering what it meant.

"A contract that you drafted so as to be unfulfillable," the Jamaican responded.

*Exactly!* Gary thought.

"That's not my problem."

Someone cleared their throat, hijacking the moment. The collective attention turned toward the tablet that the soldier standing to the left of the Jamaican man held by his side, the screen facing his hip. The soldier lifted the thing and held it out for everyone to see.

*Is that the fucking Pope?* Gary thought of the older Caucasian man on the static-filled screen. He wore a Catholic ceremonial robe, a funny hat, and an expression that was in constant flux between grave concern and altruistic compassion. He stood behind a podium set up in a smallish room. The official Vatican seal hung on the wall behind him.

*Wait a minute... How the hell do they have Internet?*

"Please forgive the interruption," the man on the tablet said rather meekly in a thick Italian accent, distorted by the weak video signal. "Our link to the satellite is tenuous, at best. If we are to perform the ceremony, we don't have much—"

"Zip it, Pontiff," Thirty-Six sneered, "grown folks are talking."

The man's words turned into distressed mumbling. His mouth had been replaced by a zipper. He panicked and slapped his hands over the zipper-mouth, his eyes darting frantically.

Thirty-Six was livid. He pursed his lips. His eyes became slits. His irises, like blackened pits, slid over to the Jamaican.

"You would have this...*clown* judge me?" he fumed. "I *reject* his authority! And I *reject yours!*"

The Jamaican waved his hand and the pontiff's mouth returned to normal. His panicked mumbling became a series of full-throated gasps and heavy breathing.

He turned to Thirty-Six and said, "Be that as it may, brother, your day of reckoning is at hand."

"I disagree," Thirty-Six replied, a roguish grin taking shape. "You see...I'm just gettin' started!"

Several of the Gatekeepers cried out and simultaneously flung their weapons to the floor as if they had become suddenly hot.

"Fucking snakes!" yelled one soldier as he kicked and stomped at his gun.

Another soldier pulled his backup weapon, a handgun, and began shooting at the gun that he had tossed to the floor like it posed an immediate threat.

The Jamaican instructed the affected Gatekeepers to "Look to your faith! Ignore his tricks!"

His words immediately woke them from Thirty-Six's suggestive spell.

The Jamaican man nodded at the soldier on his right, and the man made a subtle twisting motion that flung the long bulky gun around his torso and into his waiting hands, like a rock-star executing a perfect guitar spin.

Gary was no gun-nut, but he understood that there was nothing normal about the strangely modified, double-barreled shotgun, which looked, to him, like a hand-cannon conjured from some Steampunk nightmare.

The soldier stepped forward and pointed the steampunk cannon squarely at Thirty-Six.

"This ends here, *brother*! Now!" said the Jamaican.

Gary noticed a hint of fear flash across Thirty-Six's expression before his ego was able to replace it with something less conspicuous. He took a step back and put his hands in the air.

"Now, wait a minute," Thirty-Six stammered, his eyes locked on the barrel of the strange weapon. "Let's talk about this."

"There's nothing left to discuss."

Thirty-Six appeared to momentarily pout like a spoiled brat, denied. Gary found that slightly empowering.

"I have just as much of a right to—" Thirty-Six complained before the Jamaican cut him off.

"You forfeited your rights when you chose this path, brother." And then he turned his attention to the assistants and said, "Drop your weapons. Leave this place, and your lives will be spared."

Thirty-Six bristled, and then thrust a scowl at the men. "I'll kill whoever does," he shouted, "and make you my bitch in hell!"

The assistants traded unsure glances. One of them began to lower his aim. Thirty-Six shot a glare at the man, who began to convulse. He dropped his weapon and doubled over in pain, cradling his belly in his arms. He lurched forward and let out a prolonged wail that bounced around the room. He gasped involuntarily and groaned from deep within his soul before belching up a torrent of blood that flowed from his mouth like pressurized water from a firehose. The floor beneath him was coated in a flowering puddle that continued to spread until there was no more blood left in his body.

Then the assistant stood upright in a way that called into question whether the action was voluntary or just some last-ditch effort of discombobulated nerves. The pressure from the blood exodus had pushed his eyes from the sockets and left them empty, leaking tears of blood. The assistant swayed, and fell straight backward.

"Now!" The Jamaican yelled.

The guard on his right fired the steampunk cannon. The weapon made a thunderous sound that lagged a bit after the initial blast. A shockwave of heat-ripples spread out from the tip of the barrel.

Thirty-Six performed a sly side-step. He became like a blur and, in an instant, he was sliding in behind Handsome Hugo, who had been standing several feet away.

The blast from the cannon hit an assistant instead and swept the man off his feet. His body tumbled to rest ten feet away, a curlicue of smoke rising from a cauterized hole punched through his chest.

A trio of transparent images of the assistant, frozen mid-reaction to the gun-blast, marked his journey backward from where he initially stood to where his vacant corpse lay, like some Harvey Comics foil who laid eyes on Casper the Friendly Ghost. The first image was a full representation of the man. The second was like a map of his subcutaneous musculature, and the third was an organ-stuffed skeleton. There was a brief stutter in the images before they were suddenly snatched forward from back-to-front. The organ-stuffed skeleton merged with the subcutaneous muscleman, which bucked in response to the ethereal impact. The muscleman merged with the fully realized image. The fully realized image became animated, arching into a pain-stricken pose, and letting out a blood-curdling scream as it fizzled into nothingness, leaving only the fading echo of its death cry.

"Kill them all!" Thirty-Six commanded.

The assistants sought cover as they fired their weapons. The Gate-keepers did the same as they returned fire.

Gary scrambled on his belly toward the Gatekeeper's side of the room. He flinched and tightened at the sound of the two, nearby assistants' guns blasting away. One was using the wooden cross for cover. The other was standing in the open, in a wide-legged, TV-cop firing stance. He was the first one to drop, and he landed right in front of Gary, blocking his path.

Gary threw his arms over his head, pressed his body against the floor, and lay completely still as bullets cut through the air and rico-cheted off hard surfaces directly above him. The room smelled like gunpowder.

Down in the auditorium, the soldier with the steampunk cannon turned his aim on Handsome Hugo and Thirty-Six, but an assistant's bullet found purchase in his skull before he could pull the trigger, and he flung the weapon away as he dropped.

The Jamaican made no attempt to avoid catching a bullet or twenty as he walked out into the open space and spread his arms like a swimmer performing a breaststroke.

Across the room, the assistants' cover exploded into a cloud of multi-sized fragments of wood, metal, steel, and miscellaneous textiles, leaving them completely exposed and scrambling behind the pillars. An invisible shockwave transplanted the fragments into the nearby walls and ceiling where the click-click-clank of repeated impact could be heard over the gunshots.

Gary found himself directly in the path of the debris-shower that rained down on him, peppering his back and legs.

He panicked, slid his feet underneath him, and thrust himself to a hunched stand. With his forearms pressed against the sides of his head like earmuffs, Gary made a mad dash for the edge of the stage.


THIRTY-SIX FROWNED at the Jamaican's maneuver and, in response, waved his hand at the lights. The room became pitch-black and pock-marked with muzzle-flashes that winked at Gary from every direction. He was still on the run, having just jumped down from the stage. The sudden darkness left him guessing.

He charted a course on the fly based on his memory of the room's layout, his roving arms leading the way like antennae. He changed direction, *Please don't let me die*, on repeat in his thoughts as a distraction from the fear that tried to seize his limbs and make him a sitting duck. His foot hit a dense object that slid away under the force of his forward momentum. He overcorrected and began to stumble.

The light returned and Gary was greeted by the floor approaching fast. He threw his arms out in front of him. Landing on his hands and knees, he looked up to gain his bearings, and glimpsed Thirty-Six and Handsome Hugo darting from the room through a rear exit.

Gary gave minor acknowledgement to the fact that he had somehow made it all the way across the room, through the gauntlet of bullets raining horizontally, without being shot. Any lingering retrospective on how lucky he may have been was stopped by the sight of the steampunk cannon lying a few feet away. He grabbed it.

# 16

Gary crept down the dank corridor toward the sound of Thirty-Six's voice punctuated by crashing throughout the room. Based on the way the sound bounced down the intersecting hallway and around the corner to where Gary stood, it sounded like Thirty-Six and Handsome Hugo had stopped running.

Faded letters spelled out *PEDIATRICS* on the wall of the intersecting corridor. An arrow pointed in the direction of the voice and the hurled objects.

"The son-of-a-bitch was literally right under our noses, and you had no idea?" Thirty-Six fumed. "What the fuck am I paying you for?"

"Please forgive me, master, I don't know how I could've missed it." Hugo replied in a subservient tone, his delivery affected by the strain of heavy lifting.

"Just hurry! I'll deal with your incompetence later!"

It was hard to picture Hugo, the stoic badass, being reprimanded.

The corridor was a bit too narrow, and Gary felt as if the walls were being pinched closed behind him. The stench of mold and rot and fermented animal urine had replaced the musty gunpowder aroma from the main room. Gary could no longer hear the gunplay, which meant that it had either ended, or after navigating the maze of identical corridors and a staircase, in pursuit he had traveled far enough away from the auditorium to hear.

The décor mimicked that of the auditorium save for the occasional prehistoric toy or stuffed animal lying dirt-caked and squashed on the floor. There were doorless rooms on either side of him, every ten or so feet, empty and devoid of life. Remnants of the rooms' several uses over time—a homeless couples' suite, a drug den, a toilet —were scattered about.

Gary held the steampunk cannon in a precarious grip. It was much heavier than it looked and he tried not to stress over the nagging concern that he might not be able to withstand the weapon's recoil, or over the memory that just moments ago, he was certain that he was going to die a horrible death.

Gary ran Thirty-Six's reaction to the cannon on a mental loop as a constant reminder that the 36th Guardian of Hell could be beaten, that he held the very thing that could do it in his hands.

He reached the intersection and pressed his back against the wall just shy of the edge. Thirty-Six was still complaining and scolding Hugo for failing to sniff out the Jamaican mole.

Gary glanced down at the cannon as if to glean an extra burst of courage from it, and then, at the end of a deep breath, he peeked around the edge of the wall.

They were at the opposite end of the intersecting corridor, maybe 60 or 70 feet away. A pair of double doors just beyond their reach, their access to them denied by an improvised barrier of old rusted gurney's, rolling food-carts, and office furniture, that had been erected hastily by the Gatekeepers. A large chalk-drawing of a cross stretched across both doors. Some Arabic-like language, that Gary had never seen before, was scrawled above and below the cross. An exit sign cast a bloodshot gaze down at the two men and colored them radioactive.

Thirty-Six was hiding behind his raised arm, his head turned away from the chalk-drawing as if the sight of it caused him immense pain.

*Good to know*, Gary thought.

It didn't appear to have the same effect on Hugo, who worked tirelessly to clear the blockade.

"Hurry!" Thirty-Six ordered.

"Almost there," said Hugo.

Once he was able to, Hugo climbed over and sidled through the remaining obstacles, and then used his sleeve to wipe away the chalk drawing.

Thirty-Six lowered his arm and looked directly at the doors as the cross and the Arabic scribble were wiped to smudges. And then he stiffened in reaction to a sound from behind.

Gary wasn't ready when Thirty-Six whipped around and laid eyes on him. His mind was still recovering from the disheartening wallop of losing his advantage thanks to a nearly fossilized pill-bottle that had somehow found its way under his bare foot.

"Gary!" Thirty-Six smiled. "I *knew* you were special."

"Save it," Gary snapped back, and raised the weapon. His self-assured tone surprised even him. "You couldn't give two shits about me. I realize that now."

"No! You're wrong! I was only testing you. Like I told you before, my line of work requires the utmost vigilance."

"Line of work? You're a fucking *demon*!"

"Which is why I had to be so thorough in my vetting of you...my representative among the living."

He said it like the *representative of the 36th Guardian of Hell* was some renowned benchmark on the under-underworld corporate ladder, and that Gary should be grateful to have been mentioned in the same breath.

A millisecond of curiosity was all it took to set Gary's mind adrift on a squall of serenity, and "all-is-well" platitudes that melted away his tension and anxiety.

"You see what I'm up against?" Thirty-Six continued, manipulating his tone and cadence so as to seduce and subjugate. "They're relentless. Always watching me, waiting to swoop down and rain on my parade because it isn't in line with *Space Daddy's* vision of a perfect world. I had to pretend that you were just another victim, otherwise they would've come for you long ago."

Gary felt an unrelenting urge to comply with the smooth, silver-tongued voice, and to forfeit any thoughts of aggression toward Thirty-Six. *All-is-well... All-is-well... All-is—*

Gary was jarred awake to a breaching of his personal space, followed by a forceful jerking, and finally to the sensation of being pulled off-balance. He was able to keep from falling, but by the time he found his footing, he was no longer holding the steampunk cannon.

His reaction delayed by the prolonged aftershock of Thirty-Six's mind-fuckery, Gary seemed to move in slow motion as he turned and pointed a shocked, dumb stare at the business end of the steampunk cannon aimed dead-center between his eyes.

At the other end stood Handsome Hugo, who was holding the weapon in one hand, with his arm fully extended, his face a blur of indifference.

Gary found himself back in the realm of abject terror.

"A little late to grow a pair, don't you think?" Thirty-Six remarked, shaking his head. "Just for that, I'm gonna let you in on a little secret." Then he walked up to Gary, leaned in close to his ear, and whispered, "There is no word in the English language, or any language, for that matter, to express exactly how *insignificant* you are to me. You were simply a means to an end. Your death, and the deaths of everyone you care about mean as much to me as the sweat on my balls." He pulled back and smiled. "That's right. For what you did, I'll be paying them all a visit. I wanted to make sure you knew that."

Gary considered begging, but Thirty-Six's taunt laid bare the futility of that course of action. And even if he tried, his voice wouldn't get past the huge lump that was lodged in his throat. He considered trying to wrestle the gun from Hugo, which would likely be little more than the spark of an opening salvo, before Hugo pulled the trigger and put his body and soul to eternal rest.

"The Wraith Eater packs one helluva punch." Thirty-Six added, gesturing at the weapon in Hugo's hand as he backed away from Gary.

"The result is far from as grandiose as the death I had planned for you, but it *will* hurt. *Badly.*" He allowed a few seconds for the words to sink in, and then said in a voice filled with scorn, "So long... *Lee Revok.*"

Afterward, he nodded at Hugo, and then turned, and started walking toward the double doors.

"I'll make sure to tell Karen that you asked for her," he said over his shoulder.

Gary's posture inflated. His breathing became heavier. His chest heaved as if to gather enough air for a Hail Mary charge. He fantasized that he could reach Thirty-Six before Hugo pulled the trigger. He felt the adrenal swell at the thought of laying hands on him, of wrapping his fingers around Thirty-Six's throat and squeezing with all his strength.

At the same time, Gary expected that each passing second would be his last, and the longer he remained alive, the less he had to lose.

Just as he had built up enough mettle to step over the edge, he glimpsed something in his peripheral vision, a slight shift in Hugo's stance, and it reminded Gary of his concerns about the Wraith Eater's recoil. He pictured what the receiving end of that blast would do to his head, and suddenly it became difficult to stand. Gary squeezed his eyes shut and waited for it all to end.

Gary shuddered at the blast, and the lingering reverb. A concussive shockwave smacked him sideways and into a wall. The right side of his face, which he assumed had been blown clean off, burned fiercely. He winced at the stabbing pain in his right ear. His hearing had been reduced to a virulent tinnitus. He slapped a hand over his ear to allay the pain and was surprised to find it intact, his face seemingly undamaged. He opened his eyes.

Hugo was standing a few feet away, still locked in a firing stance, the gun pointed down the hall, at Thirty-Six, who writhed, flailed, rolled, and bucked on the floor like a fish-out-of-water hopped up on amphetamines. He groaned from deep within his chest, through gnashed teeth.

As he thrashed, an ethereal incarnation of something not quite human melted and stretched away from Thirty-Six's physical body as if being dragged out under protest, before ultimately being snatched back into it with equal fervor as the Wraith Eater's soul-extracting properties took hold. The ethereal thing melted away fell by the floor.

The thing was so wretched that Gary's initial reaction was to avert his eyes. It was like the physical embodiment of the stutter that occasionally turned Thirty-Six's shadow monstrous from. Simultaneously horrifying and piteous, the thing had skin vacuum-seal over a shriveled torso, a long fleshy neck, and a head like bald octogenarian with Micrognathia. Its face was smooth and mostly featureless save for a sphincter-like mouth and eyes like dried raisins.

Gary was unaware of the dumb smile on his face until Hugo's voice muscled in on his moment of unfiltered joy.

"Reserve your celebration," Hugo said. He was way too calm considering what had just transpired. "He is only incapacitated. We need to get him back to the auditorium."

Gary was so happy that he could've kissed Hugo, but there was still much to discern. And as long as Thirty-Six was alive, he wasn't out of the woods. With that, Gary's joy was replaced by concern as he looked at Thirty-Six wrestling with spectral manifestations of his true self.

He turned back to Hugo. "You're with *them*?" he asked.

Hugo lowered the weapon and nodded.

"But I don't understand," Gary said.

"You will," Hugo said. "In time."

# 17

"So, what happens now?" Gary asked Hugo as they stood off to the side of the busy corridor while, up ahead, Gatekeepers hurried into and out of the auditorium transferring equipment from two metal platform hand-trucks parked at the bottom of the ramp.

"Our brother will be dealt with."

*Our?*

They had given Gary one of the dead assistants' clothing to wear; a black shirt covered with bullet-holes, damp from the dead man's blood, and black pants that were wet around the crotch and stunk of urine. "These are the best of the lot," the Gatekeeper had said as he handed the clothes to Gary.

"So, you're not...human?" Gary asked carefully.

Hugo didn't answer and Gary thought that maybe he had said the wrong thing. And then a loud noise hijacked the moment.

Everyone within earshot whipped toward the sound only to find a soldier fumbling to pick equipment from a pile that had fallen off the hand-truck. The soldier froze, looked up, raised a hand to all the startled parties who had stopped what they were doing to investigate the sudden racket. "My bad," he said.

And then everyone went about their business.

"I've seen and done things that I wish I could take back," Gary said. "I know how I must look to you and your people, but if there's—"

"You will have ample opportunity to redeem yourself," said Hugo. "This doesn't end with our brother. He is ambitious in his treachery, but he is only one of many."

"Why me?" Gary then asked.

"He meant to corrupt you. To bring you over to his side thus preventing you from fulfilling your destiny."

"My *destiny*?"

"Your work will be a gospel for the digital age. Through it, humanity will find a way back to the path of salvation."

*Wait...what?*

"But I haven't even done anything."

"Not yet. But it is written, so it shall be."

Just then a gatekeeper walked up and politely interjected. "Mr. Revok. Would you like to look over the set-up before we start?"

"Huh?"

The gatekeeper gestured toward the auditorium and began to repeat himself, "The set-up, would you like—"

"No. No. I'm sorry. I heard you the first time," Gary said.

The gatekeeper led Gary and Hugo up the ramp and into the auditorium. From the doorway, he pointed out two cameras perched atop heavy-duty tripods: one in the middle of the room, pointing at the stage, and one off to the side, pointing straight up at the ceiling. Several strategically placed construction work-lights replaced Thirty-Six's traditional film lights, which were scattered in pieces across the room, along with the old camera and tripod.

Three fifteen-inch monitors, placed side-by-side, were on a folding table about twenty-feet to his right.

Gary noticed clusters of bullet-holes on the pillars and in the walls behind them. He glimpsed a pile of dead assistants in the hall-way, one of them wearing only boxer-briefs, when a gatekeeper came in from an entrance across the room. There were a few less gatekeepers than before, which suggested to Gary that they had also taken some casualties. However, there was no sign of their bodies.

In the back of the room, a pair of gatekeepers stood over four surviving assistants, who had either surrendered or been shown mercy. They were on their knees with their hands behind their heads.

Gary looked over at Hugo, who nodded as if to validate all the questions swirling around his head.

It stood to reason that Thirty-Six was the talent in this particular production, and as Gary inspected the cameras—Canon XA11 Camcorders, which he knew of, but had never used—he wished that he was preparing for any other film, with any other talent. As such, he couldn't settle into his pre-filming comfy place. Instead, he felt the same crushing dread that eventually made him dash-and-puke in the middle of the *Eaten Alive* shoot, and as he made his way over to the video village, he found himself humming his old go-to palate cleanser "*Don't Worry. Be Happy,*" to cajole the blade-winged butter-flies that wreaked havoc his gut.

There wasn't much else to inspect, but as Gary stood in front of the monitors labeled Camera #1, Camera #2, and Tablet, with his hands buried in his pockets, he pretended to scrutinize the set-up, examining the connecting wires that snaked down to a jumble under the folding table to avoid making small talk with the gatekeepers standing around him, and to keep his mind distracted from the myriad burning questions that he wanted to ask.

*How will I feel when they bring Thirty-Six out? Will I have to strength to meet his gaze or will I look away? How will he react when he sees that I'm about to film his death? Will it even matter or am I truly as insignifi-cant as he claimed?*

He felt something at the bottom of his left hip pocket and pulled it out to reveal a black cloth facemask. Gary almost smiled at the memory of his puckered-lip mask as he shoved the plain mask back into his pocket.

Without warning, the stage-right door swung open, and three men appeared onstage: two on foot and one strapped to a wheelchair shirtless, strips of grey electrical-tape over his eyes and mouth.

Watching from the monitors, Gary was surprised at just how soft and pasty Thirty-Six's body appeared, sitting slumped in the wheelchair as the gatekeeper pushed it toward the cross, the other soldier walking beside them for backup. In his mind, he always saw Thirty-Six being more fit. A phrase in Aramaic was carved into his chest with a knife, the same phrase that had been spray-painted on the door. Blood streamed from the letters.

Gary was so riveted that someone standing nearby cleared their throat to reach him. He snapped out of it ."Action," he called out, ogling the monitors.

Thirty-Six appeared to oblige the soldiers as they transferred him from the wheelchair to the cross and Gary could only surmise that it had something to do with the message carved into his chest, possibly restricting his movement, or relegating him to a semi-catatonic state. Two more gatekeepers hopped onstage to assist. Three held him down while one used a pneumatic nail gun to impale him, through the wrists and ankles, to the wooden cross.

Thirty-Six groaned from deep down in whatever it was that constituted his soul. One of the gatekeepers snatched the tape from his eyes and mouth and the vocalizations became a string of angry, desperate pleas rattled off in an otherworldly language that Gary had heard only once before.

Lifting in unison, the gatekeepers raised the cross, Mount Suribachi-style, and stood it upright. Thirty-Six's groaning intensified as gravity tugged at his bulk. His face changed from rage to anguish and back again as he continued to curse the soldiers.

He re-directed his rant when he saw Hugo and the Jamaican walk up to the foot of the stage and position themselves on either side of the cross. Moving in ceremonious fashion, they turned to face each other, spread their arms, and beckoned toward the heavens as if something was looking down on them.

Through the monitor, Gary saw Thirty-Six's eyes lock onto the camera. "This ain't over, Gary," he hissed. "Not by a long shot! They won't be able to protect you forever!"

Shocked, Gary looked away from the monitor.

"Ignore him," remarked the gatekeeper standing closest to him. "He can't hurt you now."

*Maybe not at this very moment, but what about when this is all over, and everyone goes home? What about then? What about when—*

On the monitor marked "Tablet" The priest chanted in Italian, something about "the unholiest of unholy, corrupter of morality, ravager of souls..." and "suffer eternal damnation, something, something, vilest of devils, blah, blah, blah..."

Gary's Italian wasn't what it used to be.

A wind began to blow. The smell of jasmine filled the air. Gary glanced over at the gatekeeper standing next to him, who said, "Fear not. Everything is as it should be."

The wind intensified, kicking up debris. The lights began to flicker and strobe, played tricks with the eyes. One such fleeting trick assigned the silhouette of huge, feathered wings to the backs of the Jamaican and Hugo's slender shadows.

The priest continued chanting. Gary could barely hear his voice over the wind's baritone howl that was so loud now that he had to cover his ears. He looked around the room. The gatekeepers were all doing the same. Hugo and the Jamaican maintained their ceremonious poses, only now their eyes were completely white.

Up on the cross, Thirty-Six had his eyes squeezed shut, and his head turned away from the wind and debris.

On Monitor #2, the fake Michelangelo took on a watery consistency before melting away completely. In its place, a real-time herd of swollen storm-clouds with bursts of lightning stampeded across a turbulent purple sky. The clouds merged into one collective blanket.

A bulbous shape pushed through the surface-layer and billowed downward through the surreal skylight in the ceiling. Shifting and reforming on the fly, the bulbous protrusion became a giant scowling face, made of darkened cloud-matter, its seething acrimony aimed directly at Thirty-Six, nailed to the cross. Its mouth stretched open as it came to rest face to face with Thirty-Six, who still had his eyes squeezed shut, and head turned away.

"No more," the cloud-face proclaimed in a voice so deep and rich with bass that it shook the room. And then it flicked a tongue made of lightning at the wires snaking along the floor, giving them spastic rhythm, and a voice that hummed, hissed, and crackled.

Afterward, the cloud-face dissipated into a layer of dense fog that settled throughout the room.

Thirty-Six's body seized, and then jerked into a pain-stricken arch as an otherworldly current coursed through him. His face was frozen in a tightly pinched glower, teeth clenched.

Gary could hear Thirty-Six grunting over the wind and the electric noise, which had graduated to a high-pitched whirring sound that continued to climb in pitch as if someone steadily cranked a knob from the lowest setting to the highest.

Thirty-Six's jerking spasms seemed to indicate the same and before long he was vibrating with such ferocity that it shook the wooden cross.

Steam rose from his naked torso. His skin sizzled. Epidermal bubbles rose and popped, oozing boiling pus. Sparks leapt from random areas throughout his body and ignited small fires that quickly spread. A cluster of flames climbed his pant-legs, danced on his shoulder, and planted kisses on his ear, causing it to shrivel. He whipped his head from side to side as the flames encroached on his face. Instead of feasting on his flesh, as they had done to the *Burning Man*, the flames appeared to drastically shift Thirty-Six's facial structure, and as he continued to whip his head, his face morphed through a gallery of familiar characters from Gary's life, each with their own unique interpretation of Thirty-Six's current anguish.

Within the anguish-mug montage, Gary saw his parents, several of his childhood friends from the neighborhood, his 11th Grade English Teacher, Mr. Frakes, who told him, in so many words, that he'd never make it. He saw Jonas Marks, the producer from Philly, and the German investor who had stolen his script. He saw his boss, Dave Satterfield, and even Karen, and as he watched completely thunderstruck, Gary began to understand just how intimate and enduring his relationship with Thirty-Six had been.

# 18

It felt like Gary was emerging from hell when he pushed open the front doors and walked out onto the steps of the Hudson River State Hospital. The fresh air stung and the daylight hurt his eyes, but neither was of much concern. He was still processing what had happened in the auditorium, and how it pertained to his relationship with Thirty-Six, and his role in the larger picture, which, apparently had already been written. Talk about a mindfuck.

Gary had spent the last hour standing at the foot of the stage, his attention divided between Thirty-Six's shriveled and charred skeletal remains still smoldering on the cross, and the fake Michelangelo with the sooty overlay on the ceiling, looking as if nothing had ever happened, while the gatekeepers broke down equipment and cleaned up around him.

A large, unkempt courtyard stood between the steps and the rusted front gate. Beyond it, a stretch of trees and open grassland hid the campus from the rest of the city.

The sounds of distant chaos in the streets belied the mostly peaceful morning vista. An errant flash of lightning haunted the patchwork layer of clouds that flowed smoothly beneath a boundless expanse of turquoise with splashes of pink.

Voices to his right. Gary turned to investigate and saw the gate-keepers converging around two white box-trucks parked in an otherwise empty lot on the far-right side of the building. They had the captured assistants with them as they filed into the backs of the trucks. He noticed that a few of them were staring up at the sky, so he did the same.

It took a moment before Gary glimpsed movement in the swatches of open-air between the clouds. It looked like two large birds flying in a staggered formation, but he quickly noticed the shapes of their bodies were long and human-like.

Gary felt a swell of gratitude and wonderment as he watched the shapes disappear behind the clouds. He remembered the instructions he had been given with a sense of pride.

"Take this. Continue to show them the truth," Hugo had told Gary as he handed him one of the Canon XA11s. "We will be in touch regarding the next ceremony."

"But how will I know what to shoot?"

"You are the director. That is for you to decide."

Gary looked down at the camera in his right hand, and then up toward the distant chaos coming from beyond the front gate. He took a deep breath and fished the black mask from his pocket. He put it on, lifted the camera, pressed 'Record,' and then docked the viewfinder with his eye.

With the front gate in his sights, Gary started down the steps.

# ACKNOWLEDGMENTS

Endless thanks to my co-author Andre Duza: he took this story to places I had never considered, and helped create a tale that became much grander than I foresaw. Was great to collaborate after nearly 20 years of enjoying his books. Huge thanks to everyone at Dead Sky/Death's Head Press for the guidance and advice. They helped this novella grind through the literary projector with amazing attention to detail.

# ABOUT THE AUTHORS

NICK CATO is the author of one novel and nine novellas, which include the cult favorites *The Last Porno Theater, Death Witch,* and *Uptown Death Squad.* He is the author of two nonfiction film books (both published by the UK's Headpress) and writes a film column for the recently revamped *Deep Red* magazine. He lives in Brooklyn, NY with his wife Shannon.

ANDRE DUZA is an actor, stuntman, screenwriter, martial artist, and the author or co-author of 9 novels, a graphic novel (*Hollow Eyed Mary*), and the *Star Trek* comic book *Outer Light.* He has also contributed to several collections and anthologies, including *Book of Lists: Horror*, alongside the likes of Stephen King and Eli Roth.

Andre has appeared in several movies and TV Series, including *For Life, For My Man, Final Contact, Shadow Fist 1 & 2, Blackout, Booted, Alpha Rift* starring Lance Henriksen, and *Hustle*, Starring Adam Sandler. He is a member of the Samuels Action Stunt Team lead by Action Director Robert Samuels, who is a protégé of legendary Hong Kong Action Star Sammo Hung, and the first African American member of the Hong Kong Stunt Men's Association.

# ALSO BY NICK CATO

### Novels

*Don of the Dead*

*Lovers* (forthcoming)

### Novellas

*The Apocalypse of Peter*

*The Last Porno Theater*

*The Atrocity Vendor*

*Uptown Death Squad*

*Death Witch*

*Chew Toys*

### Collections:

*Antibacterial Pope and Other Incongruous Stories*

*The Satanic Rites of Sasquatch and Other Weird Stories*

### Anthologies (as editor)

*Dark Jesters* (with L.L. Soares)

*The Gruesome Tensome: A Short Story Tribute to the Films of Herschell Gordon Lewis*

### Non-Fiction:

*Suburban Grindhouse: From Staten Island to Times Square and all the Sleaze Between*

*Dark Dreams: An Obsessive Look at Romano Scavolini's Nightmare*

# ALSO BY ANDRE DUZA

*The Undead*

**Comics/Graphic Novels**

*Star Trek: The Outer Light* (Co-written with Morgan Gendel)

*Hollow Eyed Mary*